NEED YOU

(A Daisy Fortune Mystery —Book One)

BLAKE PIERCE

Blake Pierce

Blake Pierce is the USA Today bestselling author of the RILEY PAGE mystery series, which includes seventeen books. Blake Pierce is also the author of the MACKENZIE WHITE mystery series, comprising fourteen books; of the AVERY BLACK mystery series, comprising six books; of the KERI LOCKE mystery series, comprising five books; of the MAKING OF RILEY PAIGE mystery series, comprising six books; of the KATE WISE mystery series, comprising seven books; of the CHLOE FINE psychological suspense mystery, comprising six books; of the JESSIE HUNT psychological suspense thriller series, comprising twenty six books; of the AU PAIR psychological suspense thriller series, comprising three books; of the ZOE PRIME mystery series, comprising six books; of the ADELE SHARP mystery series, comprising sixteen books, of the EUROPEAN VOYAGE cozy mystery series, comprising six books; of the LAURA FROST FBI suspense thriller, comprising eleven books; of the ELLA DARK FBI suspense thriller, comprising fourteen books (and counting); of the A YEAR IN EUROPE cozy mystery series, comprising nine books, of the AVA GOLD mystery series, comprising six books; of the RACHEL GIFT mystery series, comprising ten books (and counting); of the VALERIE LAW mystery series, comprising nine books (and counting); of the PAIGE KING mystery series, comprising eight books (and counting); of the MAY MOORE mystery series, comprising eleven books (and counting); the CORA SHIELDS mystery series, comprising five books (and counting); of the NICKY LYONS mystery series, comprising seven books (and counting), of the CAMI LARK mystery series, comprising five books (and counting), of the AMBER YOUNG mystery series, comprising five books (and counting), of the DAISY FORTUNE mystery series, comprising five books (and counting), and of the new FIONA RED mystery series, comprising five books (and counting).

An avid reader and lifelong fan of the mystery and thriller genres, Blake loves to hear from you, so please feel free to visit www.blakepierceauthor.com to learn more and stay in touch.

ISBN: 978-1-0943-8078-0

BOOKS BY BLAKE PIERCE

FIONA RED MYSTERY SERIES
LET HER GO (Book #1)
LET HER BE (Book #2)
LET HER HOPE (Book #3)
LET HER WISH (Book #4)
LET HER LIVE (Book #5)

DAISY FORTUNE MYSTERY SERIES
NEED YOU (Book #1)
CLAIM YOU (Book #2)
CRAVE YOU (Book #3)
CHOOSE YOU (Book #4)
CHASE YOU (Book #5)

AMBER YOUNG MYSTERY SERIES
ABSENT PITY (Book #1)
ABSENT REMORSE (Book #2)
ABSENT FEELING (Book #3)
ABSENT MERCY (Book #4)
ABSENT REASON (Book #5)

CAMI LARK MYSTERY SERIES
JUST ME (Book #1)
JUST OUTSIDE (Book #2)
JUST RIGHT (Book #3)
JUST FORGET (Book #4)
JUST ONCE (Book #5)

NICKY LYONS MYSTERY SERIES
ALL MINE (Book #1)
ALL HIS (Book #2)
ALL HE SEES (Book #3)
ALL ALONE (Book #4)
ALL FOR ONE (Book #5)
ALL HE TAKES (Book #6)
ALL FOR ME (Book #7)

CORA SHIELDS MYSTERY SERIES
UNDONE (Book #1)
UNWANTED (Book #2)
UNHINGED (Book #3)
UNSAID (Book #4)
UNGLUED (Book #5)

MAY MOORE SUSPENSE THRILLER
NEVER RUN (Book #1)
NEVER TELL (Book #2)
NEVER LIVE (Book #3)
NEVER HIDE (Book #4)
NEVER FORGIVE (Book #5)
NEVER AGAIN (Book #6)
NEVER LOOK BACK (Book #7)
NEVER FORGET (Book #8)
NEVER LET GO (Book #9)
NEVER PRETEND (Book #10)
NEVER HESITATE (Book #11)

PAIGE KING MYSTERY SERIES
THE GIRL HE PINED (Book #1)
THE GIRL HE CHOSE (Book #2)
THE GIRL HE TOOK (Book #3)
THE GIRL HE WISHED (Book #4)
THE GIRL HE CROWNED (Book #5)
THE GIRL HE WATCHED (Book #6)
THE GIRL HE WANTED (Book #7)
THE GIRL HE CLAIMED (Book #8)

VALERIE LAW MYSTERY SERIES
NO MERCY (Book #1)
NO PITY (Book #2)
NO FEAR (Book #3)
NO SLEEP (Book #4)
NO QUARTER (Book #5)
NO CHANCE (Book #6)
NO REFUGE (Book #7)
NO GRACE (Book #8)
NO ESCAPE (Book #9)

RACHEL GIFT MYSTERY SERIES
HER LAST WISH (Book #1)
HER LAST CHANCE (Book #2)
HER LAST HOPE (Book #3)
HER LAST FEAR (Book #4)
HER LAST CHOICE (Book #5)
HER LAST BREATH (Book #6)
HER LAST MISTAKE (Book #7)
HER LAST DESIRE (Book #8)
HER LAST REGRET (Book #9)
HER LAST HOUR (Book #10)

AVA GOLD MYSTERY SERIES
CITY OF PREY (Book #1)
CITY OF FEAR (Book #2)
CITY OF BONES (Book #3)
CITY OF GHOSTS (Book #4)
CITY OF DEATH (Book #5)
CITY OF VICE (Book #6)

A YEAR IN EUROPE
A MURDER IN PARIS (Book #1)
DEATH IN FLORENCE (Book #2)
VENGEANCE IN VIENNA (Book #3)
A FATALITY IN SPAIN (Book #4)

ELLA DARK FBI SUSPENSE THRILLER
GIRL, ALONE (Book #1)
GIRL, TAKEN (Book #2)
GIRL, HUNTED (Book #3)
GIRL, SILENCED (Book #4)
GIRL, VANISHED (Book 5)
GIRL ERASED (Book #6)
GIRL, FORSAKEN (Book #7)
GIRL, TRAPPED (Book #8)
GIRL, EXPENDABLE (Book #9)
GIRL, ESCAPED (Book #10)
GIRL, HIS (Book #11)
GIRL, LURED (Book #12)
GIRL, MISSING (Book #13)

GIRL, UNKNOWN (Book #14)

LAURA FROST FBI SUSPENSE THRILLER
ALREADY GONE (Book #1)
ALREADY SEEN (Book #2)
ALREADY TRAPPED (Book #3)
ALREADY MISSING (Book #4)
ALREADY DEAD (Book #5)
ALREADY TAKEN (Book #6)
ALREADY CHOSEN (Book #7)
ALREADY LOST (Book #8)
ALREADY HIS (Book #9)
ALREADY LURED (Book #10)
ALREADY COLD (Book #11)

EUROPEAN VOYAGE COZY MYSTERY SERIES
MURDER (AND BAKLAVA) (Book #1)
DEATH (AND APPLE STRUDEL) (Book #2)
CRIME (AND LAGER) (Book #3)
MISFORTUNE (AND GOUDA) (Book #4)
CALAMITY (AND A DANISH) (Book #5)
MAYHEM (AND HERRING) (Book #6)

ADELE SHARP MYSTERY SERIES
LEFT TO DIE (Book #1)
LEFT TO RUN (Book #2)
LEFT TO HIDE (Book #3)
LEFT TO KILL (Book #4)
LEFT TO MURDER (Book #5)
LEFT TO ENVY (Book #6)
LEFT TO LAPSE (Book #7)
LEFT TO VANISH (Book #8)
LEFT TO HUNT (Book #9)
LEFT TO FEAR (Book #10)
LEFT TO PREY (Book #11)
LEFT TO LURE (Book #12)
LEFT TO CRAVE (Book #13)
LEFT TO LOATHE (Book #14)
LEFT TO HARM (Book #15)
LEFT TO RUIN (Book #16)

THE AU PAIR SERIES

ALMOST GONE (Book#1)

ALMOST LOST (Book #2)

ALMOST DEAD (Book #3)

ZOE PRIME MYSTERY SERIES

FACE OF DEATH (Book#1)

FACE OF MURDER (Book #2)

FACE OF FEAR (Book #3)

FACE OF MADNESS (Book #4)

FACE OF FURY (Book #5)

FACE OF DARKNESS (Book #6)

A JESSIE HUNT PSYCHOLOGICAL SUSPENSE SERIES

THE PERFECT WIFE (Book #1)

THE PERFECT BLOCK (Book #2)

THE PERFECT HOUSE (Book #3)

THE PERFECT SMILE (Book #4)

THE PERFECT LIE (Book #5)

THE PERFECT LOOK (Book #6)

THE PERFECT AFFAIR (Book #7)

THE PERFECT ALIBI (Book #8)

THE PERFECT NEIGHBOR (Book #9)

THE PERFECT DISGUISE (Book #10)

THE PERFECT SECRET (Book #11)

THE PERFECT FAÇADE (Book #12)

THE PERFECT IMPRESSION (Book #13)

THE PERFECT DECEIT (Book #14)

THE PERFECT MISTRESS (Book #15)

THE PERFECT IMAGE (Book #16)

THE PERFECT VEIL (Book #17)

THE PERFECT INDISCRETION (Book #18)

THE PERFECT RUMOR (Book #19)

THE PERFECT COUPLE (Book #20)

THE PERFECT MURDER (Book #21)

THE PERFECT HUSBAND (Book #22)

THE PERFECT SCANDAL (Book #23)

THE PERFECT MASK (Book #24)

THE PERFECT RUSE (Book #25)

THE PERFECT VENEER (Book #26)

CHLOE FINE PSYCHOLOGICAL SUSPENSE SERIES

NEXT DOOR (Book #1)
A NEIGHBOR'S LIE (Book #2)
CUL DE SAC (Book #3)
SILENT NEIGHBOR (Book #4)
HOMECOMING (Book #5)
TINTED WINDOWS (Book #6)

KATE WISE MYSTERY SERIES

IF SHE KNEW (Book #1)
IF SHE SAW (Book #2)
IF SHE RAN (Book #3)
IF SHE HID (Book #4)
IF SHE FLED (Book #5)
IF SHE FEARED (Book #6)
IF SHE HEARD (Book #7)

THE MAKING OF RILEY PAIGE SERIES

WATCHING (Book #1)
WAITING (Book #2)
LURING (Book #3)
TAKING (Book #4)
STALKING (Book #5)
KILLING (Book #6)

RILEY PAIGE MYSTERY SERIES

ONCE GONE (Book #1)
ONCE TAKEN (Book #2)
ONCE CRAVED (Book #3)
ONCE LURED (Book #4)
ONCE HUNTED (Book #5)
ONCE PINED (Book #6)
ONCE FORSAKEN (Book #7)
ONCE COLD (Book #8)
ONCE STALKED (Book #9)
ONCE LOST (Book #10)
ONCE BURIED (Book #11)
ONCE BOUND (Book #12)
ONCE TRAPPED (Book #13)
ONCE DORMANT (Book #14)
ONCE SHUNNED (Book #15)

ONCE MISSED (Book #16)
ONCE CHOSEN (Book #17)

MACKENZIE WHITE MYSTERY SERIES
BEFORE HE KILLS (Book #1)
BEFORE HE SEES (Book #2)
BEFORE HE COVETS (Book #3)
BEFORE HE TAKES (Book #4)
BEFORE HE NEEDS (Book #5)
BEFORE HE FEELS (Book #6)
BEFORE HE SINS (Book #7)
BEFORE HE HUNTS (Book #8)
BEFORE HE PREYS (Book #9)
BEFORE HE LONGS (Book #10)
BEFORE HE LAPSES (Book #11)
BEFORE HE ENVIES (Book #12)
BEFORE HE STALKS (Book #13)
BEFORE HE HARMS (Book #14)

AVERY BLACK MYSTERY SERIES
CAUSE TO KILL (Book #1)
CAUSE TO RUN (Book #2)
CAUSE TO HIDE (Book #3)
CAUSE TO FEAR (Book #4)
CAUSE TO SAVE (Book #5)
CAUSE TO DREAD (Book #6)

KERI LOCKE MYSTERY SERIES
A TRACE OF DEATH (Book #1)
A TRACE OF MURDER (Book #2)
A TRACE OF VICE (Book #3)
A TRACE OF CRIME (Book #4)
A TRACE OF HOPE (Book #5)

PROLOGUE

The early morning sun shone on the mirror-calm Aegean Sea, and a light breeze rustled the palms, promising another glorious day at sea. There wasn't another person awake as Adila Saeed woke from her cabin in the servants' quarters of the yacht, donned her maid's uniform, and scaled the short staircase to the main service wing. Coiling her ink-black hair into a simple low bun, she made her way to the kitchen, too lost in her own head to notice the glamour and wealth that surrounded her.

Pink grapefruit. Her employer insisted on half a pink grapefruit in the morning, and he was a stickler. Ordinary grapefruit wouldn't do. But Adila was pretty sure she'd taken the last perfect pink one from the pantry the day before. Any bruise on the surface of the grapefruit's skin would surely be grounds for termination.

Adila gnawed on her lip as she hastened her step. She doubted that the head chef, Ramon, had been able to restock while they'd been at harbor last night. He'd been far too drunk. Her stomach lurched as she remembered the way he'd pressed up against her, caressing her backside as she'd attempted to move around him and into her quarters.

Worthless man, she thought. *Worthless men, all of them. You never can trust any of them.*

Sure enough, the head cook's drunken snores seemed to echo through the halls, shaking the very walls around her. The man was gross; the Vandiveers only kept him in their employ because the Vandiveer patriarch, Franklin Vandiveer of Vandiveer Holdings, had been fond of his crème brûlée. Ramon was never up for breakfast, leaving the rest of the servants to perform his duties for him.

As she made her way into the kitchen, she could smell the French pressed coffee already percolating.

Milla. Thank goodness for her.

"Hello!" she called to her friend, who was scurrying around the table, preparing the trays. "Do we have the pink grapefruit?"

Milla looked up, her cheeks pink from exertion. "Yes, I managed to find just one at the very bottom of the bin!"

"Oh, we are blessed today then," Adila replied, wiping a hand across her forehead. "I thought we'd be done for, for sure."

"Yes, what are the chances Ramon will ever bring the right food for these weekend excursions?" The petite blonde asked as she poured the coffee into an elegant silver service that Adila fancied must've cost more than her entire year's wages. She was lucky, though, to have this job, travelling the world on an elegant yacht. Most people in her home in Syria had it far worse, but she'd managed to escape just in time. "But it is not a problem. If I found we were out, I would've simply gone ashore."

Adila stared at her, then out the porthole. Sure enough, the marina, sparkling with several yachts, could be seen, and beyond that, upon the cliffside, was the grand Vandiveer estate. "Good heavens, I thought we were asea all weekend!"

Milla shook her head. "Ramon told me we were ordered back to port."

"But why? Is there poor weather coming?"

"Some fight between the Vandiveers."

"About what?"

Milla simply shrugged. It was true, they'd long since given up trying to comprehend the whims and frivolous actions of their employers. Fights and tantrums were everyday occurrences.

"Well, Ramon's drunk again," Adila said, shaking her head. "We'd better also make sure there's enough spirits left over this morning for all the Vandiveers."

The young Jacob Vandiveer was the owner of this yacht. He'd come from family money and was used to being given everything on a silver platter. What he wanted, he received, and if not . . . well, Adila had seen many an unfortunate employee discarded unceremoniously at port, never to be heard from again.

"Oh, I know!" Milla said. "We might not hear it from Jacob, but we'd certainly hear it from the lush."

Adila shushed her, then covered her mouth to keep from giggling.

"Oh, Jacob would never fire me," Milla said with a wink. "He loves me too much."

Adila wasn't so sure about that. It was true that Jacob's fiancé, Natasha, was barely ever seen without a martini class in hand, even in the morning. Milla made no secret of the fact that she disliked the fiancé, often joking about her odd behaviors. She gossiped far too much for Adila's liking. Adila thought it was far too risky to be biting the hand that fed her. If anyone heard . . .

She pointed to the tray. "Are these ready?"

"I'm still preparing Natasha's mimosa. You know how she likes it with fresh orange juice, and I'm still squeezing. But . . ." Milla scrutinized Jacob's tray. If they so much as forgot a napkin, there'd be hell to pay. "Two halves pink grapefruit, biscuit, raspberry jelly, black coffee, napkin, silverware, local newspaper, and oh!" She grabbed a bud vase with a rose and set it there. "This one looks all right. Yes?"

Adila nodded with satisfaction. "I'll come back for the other."

"Give Mr. Billions hugs and kisses for me." She winked again.

Adila laughed and slid the tray onto her housekeeping cart, which was stacked with fresh towels and toilet paper. She shoved off toward the service elevator, still checking the tray to make sure it was perfect. There was a slight smudge on the doily beneath the grapefruit plate. She wondered if he would notice.

Inside the elevator, she pressed the button for the master's level, eyes acutely attuned to that smudge. She ran a thumb over it, but that only seemed to make it worse.

As the numbers over the door climbed, she felt her pulse quicken. She hoped Jacob Vandiveer would be in a good mood today. If he was, he'd ignore her. When he wasn't, well . . . hell hath no fury. The only thing worse was the elder Vandiveer, Franklin, his father.

She shivered at the memory of Jacob cursing her out over a forgotten steak knife.

She was still trying to figure out what she would do if he brought up the smudge when the elevator dinged, and the doors slid open. There were two suites—he and his fiancé never shared a room, something about each one liking "their space." Adila never understood that. If you were in love, why wouldn't you want to spend all your time with that person? Of course, at only twenty-one, Adila had never been in love. Maybe she was missing something.

She wheeled the cart to Jacob's suite and rapped softly on the door.

Nothing.

She knocked again, louder. "Mr. Vandiveer?"

Still nothing. If he wasn't in there, he might already be on deck. He was athletic. Sometimes, on the few occasions that he didn't have a champagne hangover, he went on a run around the perimeter of the yacht. She listened but couldn't hear his footfalls anywhere outside. All she heard was the squawk of a nearby seagull.

She'd caught a break. Heaving a sigh of relief, she pushed open the door and went inside.

The first time she'd seen the suite, she'd thought that it was one of the most beautiful rooms she'd ever seen, with its cloud-white furniture and vast marble floors with lush, cloud-like carpeting. It was a dream. Looking at it now, she just shook her head. There was trash everywhere. The room stank of cigarette smoke and the remains of the room service that had been left on the cart in the middle of the room. Adila wondered what made them live like this. Was it the money, or the knowledge that everything would be taken care of by a maid? She couldn't imagine ever being this careless with such beautiful things.

Swallowing her disgust, she wheeled the cart through the double doors and spoke again, just to be sure. "Mr. Vandiveer?"

Again, nothing.

Her orders, when he was out, were to leave the tray and straighten up. She lifted the tray and went to place it on the table in the foyer when she looked in the mirror and realized that there was a form lying in the enormous king bed.

She blinked and whirled. "Oh, Mr. . . ."

She stopped when she realized that he must be asleep. She could barely see him over the mountain of snow-white comforters and sheets, but he hadn't stirred at all.

Adila contemplated what to do. She was about to tiptoe out, so as not to disturb him, when something made her pause.

His hand was visible, curled slightly, almost into a fist. One thing about Jacob Vandiveer was that at barely thirty-five years old and heir to a billion-dollar fortune, he was considered one of the world's most eligible bachelors. Handsome and virile, he was always on the cover of magazines with his tanned, toned body on display.

But there was something unnaturally wrong about his hand. It looked bluish in color. Lifeless.

So, she moved forward until she saw his face. His skin was unnaturally pale. Definitely blue. But it was his eyes that were the most alarming thing. They were open, pupils rolled back. His mouth was open in a silent scream.

Her mouth fell open, and a high-pitched sound erupted from her mouth, perhaps the noise that the body in front of her was trying to make. *Dead. He's dead.*

After that, her mind went blank. She backed out of the room, tripping over the edge of the bed in her haste. Before she knew it, she was on the ground, flat on her back. She'd managed to break her fall with her elbows, but the pain shot through her arms now like an electrical pulse. She lay there for a second, unsure what had happened, then turned over and got up onto her hands and knees.

Then, as fast as she could, she ran to the upper deck to find the captain.

CHAPTER ONE

Daisy Fortune sat at her desk in a rundown section of East Plainfield, New Jersey, eyeing the picture of her father on the wall as she waited for her one o'clock appointment to arrive.

In the photograph, her father, the esteemed Edward Fortune, was shaking hands with the President of the United States. Handsome and bulldog-strong, he posed on the steps of the state courthouse, fresh after breaking up a massive drug ring. National media had been there, and he'd gotten personal congratulations from the Big Man in the White House.

Edward Fortune had been a force, a well-known name across the state. Daisy had been four at the time, and yet it stood out to her as one of her first memories. She remembered how proud everyone had been of her father, and with good reason—that had been only the start of a long and illustrious career in private investigations. As a result, Daisy had gotten her nose tweaked by the president, dined with the governor, seen her father's face in enough newspapers to wallpaper the office, and enjoyed a comfortable lifestyle growing up. She and her older brother, Charlie, used to walk to this office every day after school and play with her dolls and his action figures on the now-threadbare rug.

She tapped her fingers on the blotter as she stared at the empty desks surrounding her. In its heyday, Fortune Investigations had employed over a dozen private eyes.

But that had been a long time ago. Now, thirty years after he'd gotten that commendation from the president, all but one of the desks were empty. Some of them still had typewriters on them beneath layers of dust. The place looked dirty and old. It *was* old, the HVAC always left the place ice-cold and never fully circulated the stagnant air. It smelled now of a burned popcorn mistake she'd made with the breakroom microwave a week ago. The neighborhood around the place had deteriorated, too, and now, the only businesses on the street were pawn shops and an addiction treatment center. Her father had put bars on the windows a decade ago, and yet that hadn't stopped someone from spraying a graffiti *SUCK IT* on the storefront window a month ago.

Fifteen minutes late, her one o'clock strolled in, smoking a cigarette. She stubbed it out on the front stoop and teetered in her five-inch heels as she made her way past the waiting area to Daisy. Wilma Watkins seemed the perpetually late type; she'd been a half-hour behind for her first meeting and hadn't apologized then, either. Ordinarily, Daisy might have called her out on it, but really, what else did she have going on today?

"You find anything?" she said, dispensing with greetings. She stared at Daisy expectantly, one false eyelash not quite adhering to her lid, causing it to droop into her eye.

Daisy sighed. At one point, she'd hoped to be as respected as her father. That was why she'd gone into the business, and why she'd eagerly learned everything about it. She'd wanted to make things happen. Clearly, though, things had gone wrong. Very wrong. Now, she only had a handful of clients, mostly women looking for dirt on their cheating spouses.

And Wilma clearly didn't respect her enough for even a, "Hello, how are you?"

Daisy smiled. "Hi, Wilma. How is it out there? Still freezing?" she said, hoping to coax some pleasantries out of her.

Wilma gave her a dour look and folded her hands over her bony knee. Her nylons had a run. "Don't try to soften the blow. Just tell me."

Daisy nodded and produced a folder filled with images. She handed it to her and said, "I think these say it all."

There was no way to sugar-coat it. Wilma had a husband who was, in every way, a scumbag. She really hadn't needed a private eye to tell her that. The word was practically tattooed on Don Watkins's forehead. All Daisy had had to do was trail him for thirty minutes on his lunch hour. In that time, he'd stopped in an alley to buy cocaine, then cruised on over to a no-tell motel not far away. He'd been there for less than fifteen minutes before leaving, all the while wiping his nose and tucking his dress shirt into his slacks.

Don Watkins had made her job easy. Too easy.

And that was a problem. She wanted the challenge. She wanted something juicy. But it never seemed like it was there anymore.

Wilma had no reaction as she looked at the photographs. "But who's the woman? You have a photo of the woman?"

Daisy motioned to the pile. "It's in there. Just keep going."

Wilma stopped and tilted her head as she inspected the photo of the woman who'd stepped out of the hotel room a few minutes after Don Watkins. "I don't know her. Who is she?"

Daisy cleared her throat. "Appears she is a . . . uh . . . professional."

The woman's brow knitted. "A professional? But what about his secretary? I hired you to find evidence that he was cheating with his secretary!"

"You hired me to find evidence that your husband was *cheating*. I have a reason to believe he's also had relations with his secretary. Phone calls. Unfortunately, she is out of town for the week visiting her mother in Utah, so I don't have the photographic evidence."

Wilma huffed, shoved the photos over to her, and folded her arms, baring teeth flecked with her coral lipstick. "Well, that's not what I asked for. I won't pay for another week if that's what you're insinuating."

Daisy said, "If you want evidence that he's cheating with a particular person, then . . ."

"Well, I've never been so insulted!" Wilma shouted, jumping up. "This is ridiculous. You didn't do what I asked for. I specifically asked—"

"You asked for evidence that your husband was cheating," she said, still keeping calm, though her hands clenched under the desk. "And that is what I—"

"Well, it's not good enough! I am a dissatisfied customer, and the customer is always right!" she shouted, banging her hand, with claw-like fingernails, on the metal desk. To Daisy, they looked like miniature weapons. "I demand a refund!"

Daisy shook her head. "I'm sorry, but I've provided the materials you requested, and there are no refunds."

"This is—horrible!" she cried, looking around. "No wonder you have no customers. I'm going to write a scathing review online, for sure!"

"I'm sorry," Daisy said tonelessly, running her hand though her blonde curls.

I should just close these damn doors forever. I'll bet no one would even notice, Daisy thought glumly as she watched the woman stalk away.

There was a time that such a thing would've been unthinkable. Now, Daisy didn't care that much. This place had been twisting her heart since the moment she took it over from her father when he fell ill last year. At first, she'd worked night and day to keep the business above water and to prove to him that she could handle things, so he wouldn't worry incessantly about her. But eventually, things began to slip beneath the surface. Now, there was no doubt about it. The business was dying.

It wasn't all her fault—now that everyone had a camera, people did private-eye work themselves. They didn't need her anymore. It was a different age.

But that didn't matter. Edward Fortune had always told her that the business would be hers someday. It was a treasured family heirloom meant to be protected, not thrown away like a piece of garbage. This was her responsibility.

If Fortune Investigations went under, she'd have to face the music. And she'd have to tell him, eventually.

As Wilma Watkins stormed out, Daisy followed her, then locked the door, and flipped the sign hanging from the window to *CLOSED*. It wasn't even two yet, but she hadn't had a new customer in a week. She doubted she'd have one now. Then she trailed back to her desk, sat down, opened her bank's website, and entered the information to bring up her checking account.

She winced when she saw how much money was in there. It always seemed to be less than she expected, but now, her situation was truly dire as it was barely enough to buy lunch. She had enough trouble paying rent, but with all her dad's medical bills, she'd had to put things on the credit card. Now, she couldn't even afford to make minimum payments.

Yet another thing she kept from her dad on their frequent visits.

"Oh, well, Dad," she whispered to the screen as she closed out of it. "I think it's about time we call it a day. I'm so sorry."

Tears threatened to fall from her eyes, blurring her vision, but she blinked them back.

Just in time, because the moment she regained focus, she noticed a form, standing in front of the door.

She blinked harder, sure that it was just a mirage. Usually, when someone appeared on her front stoop, it was part of a gang of miscreants with nothing better to do, or a homeless person looking for someplace to get out of the rain.

But this time, it was a beautiful woman, with pale skin and bright red lips. She looked like a glamorous movie-star of old, with her black fur coat and dark sunglasses. She paused in the doorway, dipped her sunglasses to look at the sign that listed Fortune Investigations's hours, and then peered in, pouting.

Daisy sat up straight as the woman lifted a gloved hand and rapped on the window, shaking the frame. "Anyone?" she called, looking around in distaste. She sounded like a movie star, too, with a slight theatrical accent. "Anyone in there? I'm in need of help!"

Daisy jumped out of her chair. If that was what the woman was after, she'd come to the right place.

CHAPTER TWO

The woman was lost.

As Daisy crept closer to the door, she became more and more sure of it. Though she couldn't have been older than twenty-five, she carried herself as someone much older. Her clothes were expensive, and her long, dark locks were fresh from the hairdresser. She looked as though she'd had a team of people working to make her look that good.

And why? To visit a run-down private eye in East Plainfield?

Not a chance.

By the time Daisy began to twist the lock on the old door, she was absolutely certain. The woman had gone the wrong way on the 202 on her way to hoity-toity Bernardsville and had ended up on one of the worst streets in Jersey. Now, she needed directions back to her country club. Simple mistake.

She pulled open the door, which stuck, as usual, due to the humidity in the air. Poking her head out, she was about to point the way to the highway out of East Plainfield when the woman said, her words coming fast like gunfire, "Why do your hours say you're open until five if you're not?"

Daisy stiffened. After the tongue lashing that she'd gotten from Wilma Watkins, she didn't think she could take much more. Deciding to avoid the accusation, she pointed over the woman's perfectly coiffed hairstyle. "If you just take that road—Main—you'll end up on Parkview, which will take you right to—"

"What?" the woman spat out, confused. She followed Daisy's outstretched finger with her eyes and said, "Are you trying to send me away? I spent an *hour* driving here. Well, Dylan did."

Daisy noticed the limo parked on the side of the road—it was impossible *not* to—and stopped pointing. "But aren't you looking for directions?"

"Dylan has GPS, like all normal people. I'm looking for *help*. I came all this way. Your listing online said that you were open until five. Don't tell me you're not."

Daisy stared at her, the pieces slowly coming together in her head. She'd heard of people like this before. It'd been a long time since she'd seen one, though. Actual, potential *clients*.

"Y . . . you're looking for a private eye?" she questioned doubtfully.

"Yes. Isn't that what you are?" She folded her arms across her slim waist.

"Er, yes," Daisy said, stepping aside to let the woman through. "Come in, come in."

The woman did so, removing her sunglasses with great flourish. One corner of her lip went up in disgust as her eyes did an oval about the room. She stood there and let her coat fall from her shoulders, so that Daisy, at the very last moment, caught it before it could hit the floor. It was deceptively heavy, piles and piles of fake fur that she almost got lost in as she wrangled with it, trying to put it up on the coat rack.

Once she did, she followed the woman, who left a trail of expensive scent in her wake. Something French—*Vivante.* Daisy only knew it because she'd gotten a sample in a magazine once and determined that it was perfect for her, until she went to get it at the department store and learned that it was $200 for a couple of ounces. But this woman seemed to have the pocketbook for it. She was wearing a designer black dress that hugged every curve of her statuesque model's figure, and in heels, she towered over Daisy, at at least six feet tall.

The woman spun suddenly, a question on her face.

"Oh. Right here," Daisy said, motioning around her to her desk.

The woman stepped to the chair, which was still bleeding stuffing, even though it had been bandaged and re-bandaged with duct tape. As she sat down, crossing one leg over the other in an effortless way she'd probably leaned in finishing school, she laced her hands in front of herself and said, "I am Natasha Blake."

Daisy held out a hand to shake. "Nice to meet you. I'm Daisy Fortune. I own the agency."

Far from impressed, the woman stared at her hand, then back up at her. "Natasha Blake? Of the New York Blakes."

Understanding trickled in. Daisy didn't run in rich or famous circles, but the name carried weight. In fact, growing up, it had been a bit of a household name. She pulled her hand back, unshaken. "You mean, your father is . . ."

"Errol Blake, creator and star of *Spicy Habits,* yes."

Daisy felt her mouth slide open, but she could do nothing to stop it from happening. That was a name she hadn't heard in quite a long time. *Spicy Habits* had evolved from America's most-watched cooking show in the 1970s to a line of upscale cookbooks, restaurants, cookware, and a worldwide sensation in meal kit delivery. The man's name was synonymous with amazing food. But they'd fallen off the radar, lately, after a few scandals.

"Wow. That's exciting. My mom used to swear by your dad's meatloaf. With the applesauce in it?"

"Hmm," she said, peeling off her gloves. Daisy had the feeling that the woman didn't know the recipe, since unlike her father, she didn't seem like the type to cook her own meals. "Anyway, how do these things work? You ask me questions, and I answer? Or . . .?"

"Do you have a case you'd like me to take on?" Daisy asked as she fumbled over to her seat, still doubtful as to whether the woman had wandered into the right place.

Natasha Blake stared at her in such a way that Daisy felt only three inches tall. "Obviously. You think I'd come to a place like this, otherwise?"

That was why Daisy still couldn't believe she was having this conversation. Most New Yorkers felt like they were in the center of the Universe. They rarely travelled outside the island of Manhattan, and there was no reason to do so for a detective, since there were many high-profile, successful agencies available within the city limits. There was only one reason for someone like Natasha Blake to have left New York City.

She wanted absolute discretion.

And Daisy could provide that. No problem.

"What seems to be the problem?" Daisy asked, grabbing her notepad and pen to take notes.

"It's my fiancé," she said with an annoyed sigh.

Cheating. Again. Of course, it seemed that Daisy was doomed to cases like this. Natasha Blake's man had strayed, and she wanted someone who he couldn't possibly recognize to tail him and provide the evidence.

It wasn't her ideal job, but it was money. And right now, that was all that mattered.

"I see," she said, putting pen to paper. "What's his name?"

"Jacob Vandiveer. You know, of the Vandiveer family?"

Of course she did. Vandiveer was a prominent American name, synonymous with wealth. They were in the news all the time. In fact, she'd heard something recently about them . . . but she couldn't remember what.

Daisy wrote this down. "How long have you been together?"

"Oh, quite a while. I was in his class at Yale, you see, but we didn't quite get together until we met up on vacation in Greece. And then, of course, Lesley comes in and causes all sorts of trouble. Shifty, shifty, shifty," she said, gesturing with her hands. "You know how you get a feeling? Intuition? I had it the first time I met Lesley. And he's never liked me."

Daisy looked up, confused. This case was taking a turn she really hadn't expected. "I'm sorry. Lesley is a man? Your fiancé was . . ."

"Lesley is Jacob's younger brother," Natasha said, a slightly annoyed tinge to her voice because Daisy wasn't following along.

But now, she was even more confused than ever. "I'm sorry, I must've missed something. You're here because you suspect Jacob's brother might be trying to sabotage your relationship?"

"Not trying. He *did*," she said. "Jacob was murdered last week. Poisoned."

For the second time, Daisy's mouth opened, and nothing she did could stop it. "Murdered? Poisoned?"

"Yes, on our yacht."

Yacht. Such a seemingly innocent word, and yet it struck all kinds of dark feelings into Daisy's head. She thought of Charlie, eighteen and handsome, just graduated from East Plainfield High. He'd gotten in with the wealthy crowd, and he was headed to the Ivy League himself in the fall. He'd thought that a party with some rich friends he'd made working at a local yacht club was the key to getting into that crowd.

He'd been wrong.

Daisy flashed out of the memory to find Natasha staring at her, eyes narrowed. "Am I not being clear?"

Daisy shook her head. "I'm so sorry."

Natasha reached into her clutch and pulled out a tissue, dabbing at the corner of her eyes. "So am I. Of course, there's only one reason why he would've done it. Money. He stands to inherit over one-hundred million dollars now that Jacob's out of the way. But it's terrible. Lesley blames me, can you believe it? What would I have to gain from his death? So, I'm dealing with that, and I've been . . ." She sniffled, then her face suddenly crumpled, and she buried it in her hands.

Daisy stared, feeling a little guilty for not realizing. The black dress had been a dead giveaway, but she'd completely missed it. No wonder she'd seemed rather cold. She was in mourning. As the woman sobbed, Daisy leaned over and said, gently, "Is there anything I can do for you?"

She looked up, her face trembling, eyes red, but determined. "Find out who did this. That's what you can do. I'll pay you handsomely. Whatever the cost. I need to know who did this."

"Oh. Yes, of course. I'd be happy to investigate. But . . ." She hesitated. It was only because she was desperate that she'd take this case on. The rich never sat quite so well with her since Charlie. And not only that . . . "You said the murder occurred on a yacht?"

Natasha nodded. "Yes. Right now, it's in the marina. I'll need you to come there. I'll pay all your expenses, plus whatever fee you determine, upfront." She rummaged in her clutch and pulled out a checkbook. "Just name the cost."

Daisy stared, stunned, her mind flashing back to her pathetic checking account. This seemed too good to be true, too easy, like a payday loan. Plus . . . a yacht? She'd never been on one of those.

Eyeing the woman as she dabbed her face with the tissue, Daisy asked, "What made you choose me?"

"Oh. I saw that you solved that other case, on the boat."

"Boat?" Daisy thought back, sure she was mistaken. But then she remembered that case a year ago, where motors were being stolen in the marina in Barnegat. It had gotten a tiny write-up in the local news but was hardly anything to write home about. "Those were motorboats."

The woman waved it off. "Whatever. Can you do this or not? I need someone on this, right away."

Daisy gnawed on her lip. She would've jumped on it, if not for one thing. It was likely she'd have to travel an hour east to whatever marina was the yacht was docked at. Being away from Plainfield for more than a few days meant that she'd be away from all her responsibilities. She couldn't simply drop everything. If only it was that easy. "I wonder if I might have tonight to think it over?"

Natasha stood up and began to slip on her gloves. “Fine, but I don’t like waiting.” She reached into her clutch and pulled out a business card. “Call my assistant at this number first thing in the morning. She’ll get a message to me.”

Then, with a swing of her hips, she strolled to the front of the room, grabbed her coat from the rack, and stepped into the cold without looking back.

CHAPTER THREE

It was after five before Daisy finally made it across town to Independence Court, the assisted living facility where her father had spent the past year. Despite the way she cursed every time she received a bill from the place, she liked and appreciated it. It was the best care money could buy. The nurses waited on Edward Fortune hand and foot, and he always had positive things to say about it.

She waved hello to the nurse at the front desk, who buzzed her in. "Hello, Sarah," she said to her as she signed her name in the visitor's log. "How is he today?"

The nurse smiled. "Oh, you know your father. Always keeping us on our toes."

Daisy wasn't sure if that was a good thing or not. During his good days, he was happy and charming, flirting with all of the female staff. On his bad days, though? He could be downright cruel. The problem was that it was like a game of Russian Roulette. No one ever knew what Edward Fortune they'd get.

No one could really blame him. Over the last year, he'd been through the wringer. Despite dozens of doctors and tests, his illness had yet to be diagnosed. The latest doctor had told her that he was suffering from a weakness in his limbs and confusion at times. It was the "at times" thing that was the biggest kicker, because one day, he was a perfectly fit sixty-year-old man, and the next, he could barely stand and didn't even know his own daughter's name. On those days, he'd scream and thrash in bed as though he were in the midst of being tortured.

During those times, she was the only one who could talk sense into him. She held his hands, reminding him who she was, who *he* was, until the spell passed.

Afterwards, he never seemed to remember them, which only made it harder. He never understood why he had to be watched over, twenty-four-seven, and often spoke to her about when he'd return to the agency.

She didn't have the heart to tell him that would never happen. The doctors had said so. His spells were only getting worse and more frequent.

When she reached his room, number 131, which was right across from the nurse's station, she performed her usual ritual, pausing at the door to wait to see what Edward Fortune she'd get today. He was sitting in a chair by the window, hunched over a jigsaw puzzle. She noticed he'd gotten a few more pieces since her last visit, the day prior.

"Well?" he said, not looking up from the puzzle. "Are you coming in, Diz?"

She smiled. He'd always called her Dizzy, because she'd called herself that when she was first learning to speak, and it'd stuck. *Dizzy Girl,* he'd call her since she was always tripping over her own two feet. If he remembered that, then it was a good day. She stepped in and set a bag down on the bed. "I see you're making progress."

"Slow and steady," he said, glancing at the paper bag. "You bring presents?"

She nodded and pulled out a new package of underwear. "Because you were running low."

"Ah. Jackpot," he said as she set them down near his dresser. One of the few complaints he had about this place was that the laundry service took too long. She'd recently found out he was attempting to wash his underwear in the sink and dry it in the microwave, which was a recipe for disaster. So, she'd decided to get him more. "You're too good to me, you know."

"Eh. What're you having for dinner?"

"It's pot roast night. You joining me?"

"Tempting. But I have to go home . . ." *and pack,* she thought, but didn't add it. Not yet. She had to run it past him, first. "Dad, I had something come up. At the agency."

He straightened. "A new case?"

She nodded.

He kicked out the chair across from him and laced his fingers in front of him. "Sit. Tell me."

Everything with the agency was of ultimate importance to her father. If he'd had his way, Edward Fortune would've never handed over the reins. So, whenever she had a question about a case, she always conferred with him. The problem was, nowadays, those questions were few and far between. "Well, it's a case. On a yacht."

"Yacht?" His watery eyes widened, and she could see the pain in them. She knew he was thinking about Charlie. He was only eighteen when he disappeared, and the wealthy family that had owned the yacht did everything possible to bury the story and make it seem like he'd gone off on his own. It was bullshit, though. But even though Edward Fortune had done everything to bring Charlie back, he'd run up against brick walls, again and again.

"Yes." She leaned in and whispered, "For the Vandiveer family."

His mouth opened. "I saw that on the news. They said he died, but that it was accidental."

"The fiancé suspects foul play. Something about the brother. Anyway, she wants me to look into it. She wants me to meet her, I think at the marina, tomorrow." She studied his face. "Do you think I should take it?"

"Why wouldn't you?"

She pressed her lips together, knowing he'd say that. Of course, anything for the agency. But he didn't realize that the main thing in her way was . . . well, him. She couldn't bear it if he had one of his spells while she was out of town. "It just sounds like a really big, high-profile case, you know, and—"

"And you are a Fortune. Fortunes never back down from a challenge," he reminded her, something she'd heard about a thousand times growing up. "You know when I busted that drug ring and received the commendation from the president? You know how many people told me I shouldn't get involved? That it was a waste of time?"

She smiled and rolled her eyes. She'd heard this before, about as many times. "A thousand."

"Yep. A thousand. But Fortunes don't give up. I know you won't."

She let out a sigh. On the way over, she'd been thinking about the money. Natasha Blake's promise to pay her would be everything she needed to pay for her dad's care for the rest of the year, plus clear up her credit card bills, all while leaving a little extra breathing room. It would make things so much easier.

But there was no telling how long the case would last, or how long she'd be staying at the marina at the shore. "But I won't be able to visit you as much if I'm at this yacht?"

Her father laughed. "I'm an adult. I think I can make do. Besides, the nurses say I'm doing much better. Maybe if I'm good enough, they'll spring me out of this place, and I can help you?"

He looked so hopeful. She smiled sadly. "Yeah. Maybe."

After helping him put a few more pieces into the puzzle, Daisy stood up and kissed his forehead. "Enjoy the pot roast. I should go home and get a bag packed."

He waved goodbye and she headed out to the parking lot. In her car, she dialed the number for the assistant, Miss Lynn Barnes.

The woman answered immediately. "Ms. Fortune," she said efficiently, before Daisy could say anything.

"Er, yes . . . how did you know it was—"

"You're calling to take the case, I presume."

Daisy frowned. She could've just as easily have been calling to decline. Or was it even more obvious to everyone else how desperate she was? "Yes."

"All right, you'll need to be at Westerly Point at six am sharp. Please don't be late as we'll be leaving for our destination immediately. You'll want to pack a bag as Miss Blake had informed me the business is of an indefinite length."

Indefinite length. That sent a shiver down her spine. But she would just be across the state. If necessary, she could easily return to East Plainfield. It would be fine.

"All right. You said Westerly Point? I'm sorry, I'm unfamil—"

"Yes. Just put it into your GPS. It should be about an hour from your place of business."

"Oh," Daisy said, wondering why, if she was the private eye, it felt like this assistant had done quite a lot of background work on *her*. Did Natasha Blake expect that kind of robotic efficiency from all her employees? If so, that meant there was no room for error. "Thank you. I'll be there."

"Good."

Daisy tried to say goodbye to Lynn Barnes but realized that she'd already disconnected the call. Placing the phone in the cup holder, she started the ignition on her old car, wondering what she'd gotten herself into.

CHAPTER FOUR

Daisy's adventure as Natasha Blake's private investigator was nearly over before it began.

She didn't wake up late. In fact, she'd barely slept, since she spent most of the time afraid her alarm wouldn't wake her up at four like it was programmed to. Instead, she'd spent much of the night researching the Vandiveer family and learning about their billions. When she'd finally nodded off, she'd had dreams of Jacob Vandiveer stalking her on a giant cruise ship docked somewhere in Bayonne.

Eventually, though, she'd woken up, gotten ready, and made it out the door by five.

The only problem was that her car, which was over fifteen years old, refused to start in the icy morning weather. She banged on the steering wheel a bit, prayed to the car gods, and eventually got on the road, about ten minutes late. As she drove, she plugged Westerly Point into her phone's GPS, and luckily, it came up right away.

It was a close call, driving down the Garden State Parkway, but by going ninety much of the time, she ended up making it there with a few minutes to spare. The only problem was that, as she drove in, she saw no boats at all. No water.

In fact, the only thing she saw was a large, open field and a structure in the shape of a half-moon. An airplane hangar.

As she pulled around, she noticed the jet, parked outside. The words *BLAKE ENTERPRISES* were stamped on the side. The next most striking thing was Natasha, in that enormous fur coat of hers, standing by an enormous pile of luggage as a number of men loaded the designer suitcases into the belly of the plane.

What is going on? She pulled to a stop next to the limo and looked over at her small duffle, in which she'd packed a couple changes of clothes—slacks and blouses and a few pairs of underwear. Then she looked back at Natasha, who was staring at her expectantly. *She doesn't expect me to get on that thing, does she?*

The moment she stepped out, Natasha met her at her door. "Hurry. Where are your things?"

She pulled out her vinyl bag. “Where are we—”

“That’s all?” Natasha asked with confusion, then shrugged. “Never mind. Come along.”

“I’m not going with you, am I?” she asked.

“Oh, no, of course not. I’ll drop you off at the yacht first. I’ll be staying at a hotel,” she said, leaning in. “The family doesn’t get along with me all that well, to tell you the truth. Mrs. Vandiveer was quite upset when I accused her youngest son of killing Jacob. She still hasn’t forgiven me.”

Daisy stared at her. “Wait. If they don’t know I’m coming, then how am I supposed to . . .”

Natasha huffed. “You’re the private eye. I’m sure you have some ingenuity in you to go where other people can’t and dig out the truth, don’t you? Figure it out! That’s what I’m paying you for.” She began to walk toward the airplane, her hips swishing back and forth as she sashayed in her designer heels. “By the way, Barnes sent you the deposit, yes?”

Daisy nodded. “Yes, it was . . . very good.”

More than very good. Her checking account had never been that lush, ever. She’d spent much of her sleepless evening, staring at all those zeroes.

“Good. Then can we be off?”

Daisy locked up her car and hurried after the heiress, lugging her bag. She handed it to one of the many servants who were waiting next to the plane and followed Natasha up the steps and into the jet.

She’d never seen such luxury on a plane before. The décor was all warm cream, and rather than rows and rows of cramped seats, it was set up like someone’s living room, with a few plush chairs, a leather sofa, and a dining area with a table.

Natasha threw her things down on one of the chairs. “Sit anywhere. I’m going to get some sleep. I slept terribly last night. I have this itchy rash.” She pulled off her scarf to reveal a patch of red and looked around. “Barnesy! Bring my cream and my mimosa to the bedroom! Make that two mimosas!”

A slim woman with a severe ponytail scurried out of nowhere, rushing to a small bar service near the table. “Yes, ma’am!”

With her efficient, quick moves, Daisy decided that was the woman she’d spoken to on the phone. Natasha breezed away without another look in her direction, so Daisy went over to her. "Hi, um. Miss Barnes?"

She filled a glass with what looked like far too much champagne for the amount of orange juice that was in there. "You can call me Barnesy, Miss Fortune. Everyone else does."

"Okay, Barnesy. In that case, call me Daisy." A vent over her was spitting out frosty air. She hugged herself. "How long until we arrive at the marina?"

Barnesy checked her wristwatch. "Approximately nine hours until we land, then another hour from the airport via car."

Daisy brought a finger to her ear, thinking she'd misheard. "I'm sorry. Not the whole flight. Just the flight to the marina, where the yacht is, so I can look at the crime scene."

Barnesy looked up at her, her face a mask of confusion. Daisy's stomach sank.

"You know, where I'll be getting off . . .?" she asked weakly.

The assistant lifted the glass. "This isn't a bus. We won't be stopping until we reach the marina on the island."

"Island?"

Barnesy started to walk past her, two drinks in hand. She nodded. "Rhodes."

Daisy's gut clenched. Forget about being across the state. She'd be several states away from her father now. "Rhode Island? But—"

"No. Rhodes. In Greece," she said, giving Daisy a perturbed shake of the head. "Excuse me."

She walked away at a fast clip, leaving Daisy standing there, shocked. Not Rhode Island. Not even America. Greece. She'd wanted to go to Greece, once. That blue water. Those warm breezes. A vacation there would be like heaven.

But she hadn't wanted to go *now*. Not while everything in her life was imploding. Not while her father was . . . *oh, God.*

As she stood there, in the aisle, trying to understand why she'd just been hired to travel halfway across the world, the door to the airplane sealed shut with a loud whoosh. "Please, take your seats. We'll be taking off momentarily," a voice called over the loudspeaker.

Still stunned, Daisy backed down the aisle and practically fell into a giant, plush chair that molded to her body in just the right way. Ordinarily, she'd have sunk into it and fallen asleep immediately, but now, she was too on edge. She peered out the window as the plane began to taxi down the runway, imagining all of New Jersey behind her.

"Can I get you anything, Miss Fortune?" a heavily accented female voice said.

Daisy peeled her eyes from the window and found a woman in a uniform, staring at her, smiling.

Why was she smiling? Didn't she realize that this was urgent? Daisy was on her way out of the country. Without a passport. Without hardly any clothes. Leaving her business, her responsibilities, and her father far behind.

But then she thought of the money in her account. With it, she'd be able to pay for her father's care.

"A beverage, perhaps?" the flight attendant suggested.

Daisy slowly nodded. "Uh . . . yes."

"Champagne?"

"Oh, water. Thanks," she said, collecting her bearings long enough to fasten her seatbelt as the plane began to set off for the other side of the world.

CHAPTER FIVE

Daisy was jolted awake the moment the plane touched down. Before then, she'd been having a continuation of her dream, with Jacob Vandiveer chasing her around the cruise ship, but this time, it was a lot warmer, and there were palm trees in the harbor. When she peered out the window, she saw those palm trees, as well as a sky-blue sea and white buildings, turning pink and orange under a gorgeous sunset.

It was so beautiful, she gasped. "Is that the Mediterranean?" she asked, mostly to herself.

She was surprised when the flight attendant dipped her head close to get a glimpse. "Actually, the Aegean. Beautiful, no?"

Remembering where she was, Daisy wiped at her mouth, only to find it wet. Great, so she'd been drooling on her first international flight. Not only that, but she also felt sticky and gross as she usually did when she woke up.

As she tried to fix her blonde curls into place, the double doors in the back of the plane swung open, and Natasha appeared, looking as fresh-faced as ever, wearing that scarf. She was rubbing at the red spot slightly, holding another glass, this time, of straight champagne. Draining it, she peered out the window and called, "Barnesy! Chop chop! I want to be at the Hotel Rodos before all the bars close."

Then she strode out toward the door, only remembering Daisy when she was standing by it, waiting for it to open. "Oh, Daisy. Dylan will take you to Makarios," she said, motioning to the man standing to her right.

"Makarios?"

The man grinned. "The Vandiveer estate, ma'am."

Daisy frowned. "I thought I was going to the marina, to the yacht—"

"The Vandiveer's estate contains their private marina and their yachts."

Yachts, plural. Daisy wiped her eyes, still sure that she was about to wake up from this dream. She was in a very strange and different world, that much was for sure.

As Barnesy scurried to her side, Natasha said, "If you need me, you have Barnesy's info. Just give her a ring and she'll get in touch. Best of luck!"

The door opened, and she swept out, followed by her entourage of helpers.

So that was it. Daisy felt a little like she'd been thrown to the wolves, but in a way, Natasha was right. She wasn't a police officer. Like Edward Fortune had always said, *The advantage of being a private eye is that you're not official. Criminals will trust you more than someone in the police. So use that.* It was up to her to weasel her way into the family and get people to let their guards down, so that they'd admit things that others normally wouldn't.

The only question was, how?

She had it in her mind that she'd maybe show up at the place, asking for a job, and wiggle in that way. But as she gathered her bags and set off for this place called Makarios, she still wasn't sure exactly what her plan of attack would be.

Dylan lowered the divider between them and said, "You've never been here before."

At that moment, Daisy realized that she had her nose pressed against the window, trying to see everything of the scenery before the sun fully sunk behind the horizon. She said, "I've really never been anywhere before. My family wasn't big on travel."

"Oh, well, you'll love Makarios. I've been all over in the employ of Ms. Blake, and I don't think I've ever seen any place so lovely. It's a regular paradise. You're in for a treat," he said, winking at her from the front seat.

She wondered if she'd even get the chance to see it in daylight, or if they'd throw her out on her ear before she had a chance. "So, you know the Vandiveers?"

He nodded.

"Let me ask you . . . what are they like? Are they . . . reasonable people?"

He scoffed. "Well, that Jacob was something else. Definitely spoiled, definitely expected everything to be given to him. He'd get on your case if you even looked at him the wrong way. Lesley's a bit better, but not much. I think they learned it from that father of theirs. He's a typical businessman. Doesn't care about feelings, just the bottom line. That wife of his is a sweetheart, though. If you want an in, go through Myrtle."

She took this information in, wondering whether she'd even have a chance to meet a Vandiveer, or if she'd be blocked at the door by one of their many servants.

As she was practicing a script in her head, an iron gate appeared in her view. It seemed to stretch on forever, the size of a small country, lined with palm trees and gas lamps, blazing at regular intervals. The lawn beneath it was manicured and dotted with purple flowers.

Daisy had just lost interest in it when Dylan said, "This here is Makarios."

When she looked up, the trees surrounding it seemed to part, and she saw a sprawling estate of white walls with various balconies and outbuildings, all with uniform, terra cotta roofs. The trees and shadows obscured most of it, so she couldn't tell quite how large it was, but she had a feeling that it was much bigger than what she could see. "Oh, it's lovely."

He pulled in front of the gate. "I'll wait to make sure you're okay."

"Thanks," she said, stepping out and walking to the guardhouse. There was a man sitting at a computer, looking bored.

He glanced at her, then shooed her away and said something angrily in a language that must've been Greek.

"Um . . . I'm looking for a job? I don't speak . . ." she began, looking over at the computer screen. It wasn't a computer screen—he was watching a soccer game.

"Round back," he muttered, annoyed.

At first, she didn't quite understand, but then the gate buzzed and clicked open.

"Follow the path to the right," he grumbled.

"I will, thanks!" she said, giving Dylan a thumbs up. He returned it and started to pull away as she went through, following the path. Only after walking about a quarter mile did she understand exactly how large the estate was. She passed several buildings, which were scattered along the hillside. Taking the steps down toward the sea, she swatted at an insect in the dark and found it was almost the size of her hand. "Yuck!"

"Who's there?"

She turned to find a man in a tuxedo, striding toward her. He was tall, with silver hair, holding a glass of champagne and looking a bit rumpled, despite his attire. The bow tie was hanging and his shirt was a bit open, and he seemed to slur his words when he said, "What do you think you're doing here?"

"I'm looking for a j—"

She barely got a word out before he put a hand on her shoulder, spinning her around. "Oh, no you don't. We're not falling for that. We've had about a hundred people just like you, banging down our doors, wanting to know what happened with Jacob. You people can't leave well enough alone, can you?" he spat. Then he tilted his head to get a better look at her. "You're American?"

She nodded.

"What are you, a reporter?"

She contemplated telling him the truth, but that probably wouldn't get her any further.

"Well, that makes no difference. There's no story here, so Nosy Parkers like you aren't welcome. Jacob's death was a suicide, and that's all there is to it. We'd like our privacy."

A suicide. She hadn't heard that before. Yes, Natasha thought that it was a murder, but the official word in the news was an accident. Daisy couldn't blame him for wanting time for the family to mourn if that was the case. It made the whole thing seem so much sadder.

"I'm sorry, I just—"

"Don't waste my time. I want you out of here, immediately. The guards at the front were supposed to tell you that. Come with me." He nudged her toward the gate with surprising force. They walked in silence until they reached the guard post. He barked, "You!"

The guard looked back lazily, then immediately straightened and let out a strangled cry. He stood up and removed his hat. His voice cracked as he said, "Yes, Mr. Vandiveer?"

She stared at him. Mr. Vandiveer. The big man. Jacob's father. The billionaire himself. Her stomach sunk. If this man, the man who owned all this, had practically shoved her off the property, what chance did she have to stay?

Vandiveer stood with his hands on his hips. "You let this woman through?"

The guard eyed Daisy as if he'd never seen her before. "Uh . . ."

"I thought I told you, no one seeking employment. Have I made myself clear? We're locked down."

"Yes, sir." He quickly retreated to the guard post to unlock the gate.

When it was unlocked, Daisy stepped through, feeling dejected. If she couldn't make this happen, she'd have to give the money back. And that meant she would've come all this way for nothing.

She looked back, but the Vandiveer patriarch motioned her to keep on walking.

So, she did, through the darkness, not knowing where she would go from here. Her phone didn't have much of a charge left, but she used the last few bars she had to dial Barnesy.

The phone rang and rang, and then a voice message came on, "You've reached the private secretary of Natasha Blake. Please leave a message, and your call will be returned . . ."

At the beep, she started to speak, but didn't know what to say. *Hi, it's Daisy, I'm a complete failure. Please pick me up so I don't die on a strange Rhodesian street corner?*

How pathetic. Her father would not approve. She was a Fortune, after all. They didn't turn away from challenges. Their attitude was that obstacles were made to be overcome.

Ending the call, she stepped along the sandy street, following the iron fence, wondering what to do. She could try to scale the fence, but it was high, and the points atop it looked lethal. Even if she did get over, what would she do, then? She couldn't simply sneak about, trying to interview witnesses.

Maybe it was impossible. She had enough money in her account to get a hotel room for the night—at least, for now, until Natasha Blake insisted on a refund. If she had to fly herself back home, that would be thousands of dollars.

Sighing, She ran both hands down her face. "I knew this was a mistake," she mumbled. "You heard it yourself. It was a suicide. No one in that house is going to believe it if you tell them that you have reason to believe Jacob Vandiveer was murdered."

"I would," a voice said suddenly.

She jumped. Until that moment, she'd been sure that she was alone. Now, as she looked around, she saw two eyes peering through the slats of the fence. As Daisy moved closer, she made out the individual features of the woman. She had short, reddish hair, heavily styled into a fashionable bob, and she was wearing a lot of gold jewelry and a fancy capri outfit with sequins on the hems.

"I was just sitting at my gazebo, enjoying the evening as I usually do, when I saw you. Do you have information about what happened?"

she asked, her hands wrapping around the bars. As they did, the diamond on one of her fingers caught the light. It was the size of a robin's egg.

"I might," Daisy said, moving closer until she was only a few feet from the woman.

"Oh, don't play coy with me. If you have information about my son, I want to know it."

Daisy blinked, her suspicions confirmed. "Myrtle Vandiveer?"

"That's right. And I know my son better than anyone. He never had a suicidal thought for a moment." The woman tilted her head. "You know who I am. And yet I know nothing about you?"

"I'm Daisy. Daisy Fortune."

"An American, I see," she said, pressing her lips together. "What brings you out here? Did you know my son?"

"No," she admitted, tired of hiding the truth. It didn't seem to matter anyway. If Myrtle Vandiveer was suspicious of her son's death, maybe she'd want help in finding out what happened. Maybe she wouldn't have to lie. "I'm a private investigator."

The older woman's eyes widened. "Are you?"

"Yes," she said, stopping short of saying who'd hired her. If Natasha Blake hadn't wanted to stay at Makarios, then she wasn't welcome. She said she hadn't done herself any favors by accusing the younger brother. Daisy decided to keep that quiet, for now. "I heard about the case, and certain people who knew him didn't believe it was suicide, either."

"Did they?" the woman said in surprise, and Daisy bit her tongue, hoping she wouldn't ask who'd been saying such things. "Well, I can't deny. My son was a bit of a scoundrel. Made his enemies. He was also spoiled rotten, partially my doing, I'll admit. There are plenty who didn't like him. But he didn't want—or deserve death. Not at this young an age."

Daisy nodded, a bit mystified that the woman could be so collected over the death of her son. According to the articles, it had happened a couple of weeks ago. Had that been enough for her to get over such a loss? Or were the rich used to keeping their emotions in check because they never knew who was watching? "I wanted to offer my services. I want to get to the truth."

Myrtle clapped her hands. "Oh, that's splendid. The man I have on it is foreign. French. He's good, but he gives me the creeps. I'd love to have an American girl on it. And you look just the type. Inquisitive. Sharp. I am sure you'll find out more than him."

"Y . . . you already have a PI looking into it?" Daisy stammered, confused.

"Yes, that's right. I hired him the moment it happened. He came highly recommended, but he's a little too chummy with the local law enforcement if you ask me." She rolled her eyes. "They're absolutely worthless. Made a complete mess of the crime scene. It's nothing like America, that's for certain."

Daisy nodded. "Well, I can see if I can add anything, if you'd like."

"Your help would be welcome. Most definitely."

She pointed to the gatehouse. "Your husband didn't seem to want any guests in the house. I met him earlier."

"Oh, him?" She waved him away as if he were nothing. "Frank is suspicious. He doesn't trust anyone. I, however, recognize that no man is an island. We all need help, from time to time. What can I do to help you, help us?"

Daisy looked up and down the thick, wrought iron gate between them. Prisons didn't have so much security. "Well, first . . . do you think you can let me in?"

CHAPTER SIX

Daisy gasped again and again as the matriarch of the Vandiveer family led her around the fortress of an estate. The place was grander than any she'd ever seen, so grand that she felt like a tourist exploring it, constantly fighting the urge to snap photographs of its opulence.

Myrtle Vandiveer, though, true to the rumors about her, was as cheery and pleasant as she looked. She was short and a bit portly but had a pretty face and exquisite make-up and jewels, the tell-tale sign that she was well taken care of. There was also a trace of a Southern accent in her voice as she said, "Makarios means 'you are blessed,' but I think I am blessed to have met you, Daisy, dear. What were the chances?"

Daisy smiled as the woman led her past a courtyard filled with mosaics and a giant fountain with a statue of a naked woman at the very center, pouring water from a large vessel. As Daisy marveled at it, Myrtle said, "This guest cottage isn't in use. You're welcome to stay here."

Daisy whirled to see a home that looked nothing like a cottage. It was a castle. "All this—for me? Are you sure?"

Myrtle stepped through an archway to the front door. "Well, we're Americans. We do everything big. We don't have anything smaller than this."

She pushed open the door to a brightly lit foyer, open to the outside. It was made to look rustic, with Cycladic blue and white curved surfaces, and another, smaller fountain in the center. A small, blonde woman was fluttering about a warm, welcoming living area with wicker furniture, straightening.

"Oh, Milla," Myrtle said.

The young blonde seemed to jump slightly, and her hand went to her heart. Then she let out a sigh of relief. "Oh. Hello, Mrs. Vandiveer," she said in an accent that Daisy couldn't quite place.

Myrtle motioned Daisy in. "I'm glad you're here. This is Daisy."

The woman bowed her head slightly, as if addressing royalty. "Hi," Daisy said, uncomfortably bowing her head in response.

"Daisy, this is one of our housekeepers, Milla. She can get you settled in here." She checked her watch. "Now, I must be going. Franklin—Mr. Vandiveer— is probably wondering where I am."

She gave Daisy a pat on the shoulder and swept out of the room without another word.

Daisy stood there, marveling at the splendor around her. This one room of her guest quarters was bigger than her apartment. And had she ever expected she'd live someplace with her own fountain? It felt like a dream come true.

Milla walked past Daisy and, to her surprise, grabbed the bag off her shoulder. "You must be tired. I just put fresh sheets on the bed in the master bedroom. Come this way."

As she was led through another arched hallway to the bedroom, Daisy decided that this was a perfect time to ask questions about the lay of the land and of the other people who Jacob was in touch with on a regular basis. As Milla opened the door, Daisy said, "Wow, so you're a housekeeper for the Vandiveers, huh? How long have you been at it?"

Milla shrugged as she turned on the lights. "A year. I wanted to move somewhere warmer than my home in Norway. So, here I am. Do you want me to turn down the bed?"

Daisy stared at the king-size bed, covered in a white, crocheted duvet and lace pillows. There were vases of fresh, red flowers on every surface, and the window was open, so the place smelled like the ocean breeze and bougainvillea. She could hear the distant sound of the waves crashing on the shore. "No, this is beautiful, though."

"Of course. Mr. Vandiveer is very particular. He likes things just so."

Was it Daisy's imagination, or was there some bitterness in the young maid's voice? "Is that right?"

She nodded. "I'll bring you a breakfast tray in the morning and leave it on the patio."

Daisy thanked her, dazed by the royal treatment. Was this what it was like to be obscenely rich? Ordinarily, had this been a vacation, Daisy would've been dancing with excitement. But she had a job to do. So, when Milla said, "If there's nothing else . . ." and went to step out of the room, Daisy shouted, desperately, "Wait!"

The pretty, pale girl with the blonde braid stopped. "Yes?"

Daisy blushed at the way the girl was looking at her. She looked concerned as if she might've done something wrong. Did all the staff walk on eggshells like that?

"Sorry. I just wanted to ask a little bit about this place."

The maid hesitated in the doorway, clearly surprised by the question. "Like, what did you want to know?"

"Well . . . how many servants do the Vandiveers employ?"

She blinked. "Oh . . . many. Housekeepers, they have twenty-three of us. But there are cooks, gardening staff, the marina, the drivers . . ." She pressed her lips together, thinking. "At least a hundred of us, I'd say."

Daisy nodded. That would be a lot of people to go through. "And how many servants usually work on the Vandiveer's yacht?"

"Which one?"

Of course, they'd have more than one. "Which is the one that Jacob usually used?"

Her brow wrinkled. "The one he was on when he died is the *Fantasea*, if that's what you're asking." It was, but obviously, she hadn't wanted to come right out and say it. Now, Milla regarded her with suspicion. "Only a few stay on there when it goes out to sea, but when it docks at the marina . . ." she shrugged.

"Was anyone else on the yacht with him?"

Milla frowned. "I'm sorry. Mrs. Vandiveer didn't say who you are. Are you a friend of hers?"

"I'm a private detective."

Her eyes widened. "Oh. What happened to Gireau?"

Gireau. That must've been the French detective Myrtle had spoken about. "Oh, he's still around. I'm just poking about, trying to get a little more information so that we can find out what happened as quickly as possible."

The girl sighed, and her shoulders slumped. "Oh, that would be good. I was on the yacht that day, and it was . . . terrible. Just terrible."

"You were?"

She nodded. "I did not see the body. My friend, Adila, found him. The doctors say that it was suicide, but I do not know. Adila said he looked . . . wrong."

"Wrong, how?"

"I don't know. You'd have to ask her. They were out partying, all night, as they usually did, on deck. They drank very much. He and his friends, his brother, and his fiancé? They do some wild things. So, I don't know . . . would a man party like crazy and then kill himself? If anything, it would be more of an overdose. Drugs, reckless behavior, you know."

"Really?"

She nodded. "Yes. The whole family was very reckless if you ask me. Jacob was into everything. Maybe he got something bad. And, of course, his parents wouldn't want anyone to know if that was the case."

That made sense, but Natasha Blake hadn't mentioned drugs. Or a party. Or anything of the sort. "Did he have enemies? Fights with anyone?"

She shrugged. "I suppose. He knew a lot of people. I can't say that many people liked him, and I think he was used to keeping secrets. But I stayed out of all that. We're all on edge. Mr. Vandiveer has been very careful about who is on the property. He let go of half the staff after it happened. He and his son were always quick to fire staff, but this made him just—break. And then he closed the gates on this place and told us not to talk to the media or anyone." She shuddered. "It's not been a very pleasant few weeks."

"I can imagine," Daisy said with a yawn. It had to have been the jet lag, because instantly, she was exhausted. "Well, thank you for all of this. I suppose I should turn in."

Milla gave another small bow and motioned to a button on the night table. "If you need anything, just press the call button. It rings to the servants' quarters, and there's someone always available."

"The servants' quarters?"

"It's three buildings over, between the main house and the patio. If you hit the long set of steps to the ocean, you've gone too far."

Daisy frowned. Maybe it was that she'd come here at night, but she had little idea what lay outside her front door. It had all been building after shadowy building, among many flowering bushes and palms. In fact, she doubted she'd even be able to find her way to the front gate.

"It's easy," Milla said, noticing her confusion. "The whole estate is set up like a giant diamond. If you follow the main road, you will not get lost."

"Okay," she said doubtfully. She'd never had the best sense of direction, and often got lost in East Plainfield, even though she'd lived there her whole life. She walked Milla to the front door. "Thank you for everything."

When she closed the door, she walked to her bed and sat down on the edge of it, surprised at how soft it was. Lying back against it, she felt like she was resting on a cloud. She closed her eyes, thinking of Jacob Vandiveer partying out on the deck of his yacht. Had he taken drugs and overdosed? Or was he a victim of some of the secrets he'd kept?

Tomorrow, she would try to find out. It was the last thought that went through her mind before she fell asleep.

CHAPTER SEVEN

The following morning, Daisy leaned back in the wicker chair on the patio of the guest house and breathed in the ocean air.

It was only eight in the morning, but it was already bright, with a light, cool breeze. As promised, a tray had been left on the patio table, with coffee, juice, eggs, bread, yogurt, pastries, honey, and the most perfect pink grapefruit she'd ever seen in her life. It was all provided on dainty doilies on what must have been an extremely expensive silver platter. As she scanned the blue shoreline, the many fishing boats coming into the harbor, and the rocky coastline, she felt a million miles away from that drab office in East Plainfield.

This was the closest to heaven she'd ever been.

And yet, the specter of death hung heavy in her mind as she scanned the many yachts lined up in the marina. She spied the *Fantasea*, the biggest and flashiest of them all, sleek and white, with dark windows and an air of superiority to it. Something had happened to Jacob Vandiveer on that ship, and now, he was dead.

This morning, she hoped to find answers.

As she was sipping the last of her morning coffee, a voice called, "Yoo hoo!" from inside. A moment later, Myrtle appeared, wearing another flashy ensemble: a teal blue, gauzy caftan over a Hawaiian-print bathing suit, a straw hat with a wide brim, and sandals. "Good morning, my dear. How did you sleep?"

"Fine, thank you."

"Splendid!" She clapped her hands again. "I've been talking you up to the husband. Oh, Frank's suspicious, but I think he's starting to warm up to you. He was never too fond of Gireau, poking about. But a beautiful young woman like yourself? I think he'll warm up to you much easier."

If only Daisy believed that. But her first interaction with Franklin Vandiveer hadn't exactly gone well. In fact, he'd practically dragged her off his property. "Is he starting to think that his son might have been murdered?"

She frowned. "Well, no. He thinks I'm crazy. At least, that's what he says. But I think he doesn't want to admit it. He wants to move on. But I—" She sniffled, and her voice nearly cracked, but she swallowed it back, took a deep breath, and regained her composure. "I can't. He's my son. And I will not be able to move forward without the truth."

"I understand," Daisy said, trying to think of something else, some words of comfort to offer before the conversation turned awkward.

But Myrtle Vandiveer clearly didn't do awkward. She reached into her beach bag and pulled out a piece of paper. "I thought I would bring this along so you could see. This is the official coroner's report. You'll note suicide, overdose of fentanyl. Rubbish, really. My son did not abuse drugs."

Daisy read it. It seemed to go in line with what Milla had said about him being a big partier. There was no notice of anything from years of sustained drug use, but there was mention of a damaged liver associated with a life of heavy drinking. "It says that he was drinking. He had a pretty high blood alcohol content as well."

"Yes, well. He liked to drink. The police said that the drug was found at the bottom of his glass."

"Did they?" That was interesting. It wasn't like he'd injected himself with it, which would be more indicative of suicide. Anyone could have poisoned the glass while making the drink. "Were you on the *Fantasea* with him that night?"

"Oh, no. I don't care for the sea, to tell you the truth," she said, taking the report back. "He and his fiancé were having a joint bachelor-bachelorette party with friends and some family."

"So, your husband wasn't there, either?"

"No," she said, studying the tray. "Speaking of, if you're done with breakfast, I'd like you to come to the main house and meet everyone."

Daisy pushed out of her chair and followed Myrtle out of the guest building. As she walked, she tried to make sense of the compound and where everything was, but Myrtle chattered along incessantly until Daisy was hopelessly lost, once again. The main building had the same white walls and cornflower blue accents, with imposing turrets everywhere and a brown tile roof, just like the rest of the houses, but it was absolutely enormous. As Daisy stood in front of it, watching it stretch off into the distance, she couldn't see where it ended. "This is impressive."

"Hmph," Myrtle said with a roll of the eyes. "Give me a one-room cabin and a cozy night by the fire, any day. That's how I grew up, in Tennessee, and I have to tell you . . . I miss it."

"Really? How did you meet—"

"Ol' Moneybags? In college. I was poor, but smart. On scholarship. We fell madly in love," she said with a twinkle in her eyes. "Which is not something that happens nowadays."

"What about Natasha?"

Myrtle stopped walking, and her dreamy smile melted from her face. "Natasha? Why would you ask about her?"

"She was his fiancé, yes? She was on the ship with him when he died, right?"

By the time Daisy finished asking the question, Myrtle looked positively spooked. Her cheeks were red, her eyes wide. "Yes. Yes, she was."

They were now standing in a courtyard with yet another fountain. This one, too, was open to the outside, but much larger than the one in the guest house. Airy corridors stretched out from each side, heading to different areas of the house. Somewhere, a bird twittered. "Didn't you like her?"

The woman hesitated. "It wasn't that I didn't like her. She was just—I don't know. Someone with strong opinions. She took a bit of getting used to. If my sons like a woman, I do my best to be supportive. To find what it is that they saw in her. But with Natasha . . . well, I had a feeling that they were too alike. Jacob was spoiled, and so was she. They'd get in some terrible fights." She shook her head. "But she came from a good family, and so I tried to accept it. I thought we were getting along just fine. That is, until he died."

"What happened then?"

"Well, she was the one who first got the idea of hiring a PI in my head," Myrtle said, lowering her voice to a whisper. "She made no secret of the fact that she thought Jacob had been done in by my youngest son, Lesley. She insisted that it was murder!"

"Murder!" a voice called from down the hall.

They both turned to see Franklin Vandiveer striding toward them. He was wearing a white linen suit and a loud, flowered shirt, opened at the collar. His full head of white hair was impressive, combed back from his tanned face. When he caught sight of Daisy, he let out an enormous sigh. "So, you're the newest PI that's going to put to rest my wife's silly murder theories, is that it?"

Daisy opened her mouth to speak, unsure if he even realized that she was the one he'd given the boot to last evening.

"Well, have at it," he said before she could re-introduce herself, stepping aside as if giving her access to the entire house. "It's a ridiculous assertion, I'm telling you now. If you find anything to support it, I'll eat my hat."

She was still trying to introduce herself when he strode off, opening a wooden door in the foyer and pulling out his golf clubs.

Then he stepped out without so much as a goodbye.

Myrtle gave her an apologetic look. "That's my Franklin. He is always in a rush to get everywhere. I suppose it's that attitude that made him his millions."

"But the Vandiveer family has always been wealthy for generations," Daisy pointed out.

"Oh, yes. But Frank made his fortune, independent from the family money," she explained, guiding her down the hallway, into an open room with a grand piano and walls covered with bookcases.

"Sit, sit," she urged, pointing to a pink chaise. "Now, how can I help you? I'll have tea brought in. You need strong tea to do any thinking around here. I'd have you talk to Lesley, but I think he went out golfing with his father. I can give you a tour of Jacob's quarters? Or perhaps you want to visit the yacht to search for clues?"

"Actually, I'd love to talk to the maid who found the body, first?" Daisy said, pulling out her notebook. She'd jotted notes there last night, but now, they were almost illegible. "Milla told me her name was Adele?"

"Adila. Yes. Darling girl. Speaks good English for a foreigner." She stepped to the edge of the room and pressed a call button, waited a moment with no response, and then called, "Milla!"

Again, no response.

Myrtle went to the door. "I'll go fetch her. And that tea!"

Daisy wandered about the room, looking at the photographs spread out on the back of the piano. There was one faded portrait of a much younger Myrtle and Franklin Vandiveer, on a beach, with two young teenagers in swimming trunks. She moved in closer, looking at the picture of Jacob. She recognized him from the photos she'd seen in the news—even then, he was handsome, with an athletic frame.

Lesley, however, was pudgy, with love handles and an unfortunate bowl-shaped haircut. Nevertheless, the two boys had their arms around each other. They looked like the best of friends.

But Daisy knew that things changed. Adult troubles had a way of taking over people's lives. Maybe something between the brothers had festered, leading Lesley to murder his older brother. Maybe he'd simply been after the money.

If that was the case, though, he'd certainly gone to drastic measures. And for what? Unless he was playing the long game, it made no sense. Myrtle and Franklin Vandiveer weren't even sick. There was no reason to kill Jacob Vandiveer for the money.

So, if Lesley was the killer, it had to be for some other reason.

That was, if it was even murder, in the first place.

Her mind was so busy cycling through various scenarios and motives that she didn't realize anyone was in the room with her until someone cleared her throat.

She turned to find a slight woman with dark skin and a dark maid's uniform, holding a tray. "Mrs. Vandiveer asked me to bring this to you," she said with a heavy accent. "Tea."

"Adila?" Daisy asked as the young woman slid the tray onto the coffee table and began to pour the tea into dainty china cups from a silver carafe.

"Yes, Mrs. Vandiveer said you'd want to talk to me," she said, placing the carafe down. "Honey?"

"That's fine," Daisy said without giving it much thought. She wasn't in much of a mood for tea right now, anyway. She wanted to hear this woman's story. "You found Jacob?"

She nodded and passed the teacup to Daisy, then sat on the edge of a high-backed chair as if she didn't want to disturb it too much. "I did," she said, without much emotion. "It is not the first dead body I have seen. I escaped my hometown because I see many dead bodies. People torn apart by bombs. But I did not expect to see young Jacob dead. Not him."

"When did you find him?"

"Early in the morning. I brought him his breakfast. I always did. I knock first, and if he doesn't answer, I bring it in and straighten his room. Sometimes, he like to run on deck in the morning. Jacob was not very neat. He threw his things around. Did not take good care of nothing. So I would clean and leave him his breakfast." She dug her hands into the pockets of her apron. “But he was still in bed. Blue. Eyes open. He was dead. I know that right away. So I run out and go to the captain.”

“When was the last time you saw him alive?”

“The night before. On deck. They had a party. I served dinner, but when I went to bed after, I heard them on deck.”

“Who was this, on board, at the time?”

She began to count off on her fingers. “Jacob, Natasha, Lesley, his *cousin*—they call her Coco—some of his friends from Yale, some of her friends from L.A., I don’t know their names. They were all very fancy people. There were about ten of them.”

Daisy nodded, glancing at the photo of the two boys, standing together. “How long have you been employed as a maid?”

“A few months.”

“And what did you think of Jacob?”

Her nose wrinkled. She looked around and whispered, “He was not a nice man. I do not think any of us liked him. He treated us badly. Like we were nothing.”

“So, when you saw them, were they doing drugs at all? Did you see any drugs as you were straightening up?”

“Not in his room.”

“But in others?”

Adila nodded and pointed to her nose. “Natasha.”

“Cocaine?”

Adila nodded.

That didn’t explain the fentanyl that had been found in his system. “So, there’s no reason for you to think it was an overdose, then?”

“Oh, no. No, he was murdered. I am sure of it.”

Daisy raised an eyebrow. “How can you be so certain?”

Adila shrugged. “Just that he was not a nice man. And he was the type of person people would want to be dead.”

That wasn’t exactly convincing evidence pointing to Jacob’s murder. Daisy said, “If you think it’s murder, do you have any idea who might’ve done it?”

She almost—but not quite—smiled. “I know so many who might have. Who did? No. I do not know. Someone on the yacht. But not me. That is all I can say.”

Daisy paged through her notes. "Milla told me there are only a handful of permanent staff on the yacht. And you said there were about eight guests, is that right?"

Adila nodded.

Looping her curls into a ponytail, Daisy took her pen and began to write down the names. Her first step was to compile a list of suspects. She wrote:

Lesley

Natasha

Milla

Adila

Coco

Excluding the victim, that left only a few more suspects. Now, she just needed to fill in the blanks. "Do you think you can give me a list of the other staff aboard that day?"

"Of course." She reached into her pocket and pulled out a paper, handing it to her. When Daisy stared at it, confused, she said, "The other PI asked the same."

Right. Gireau. Eventually, she'd have to meet up with him and compare notes if he was amenable. "Do you happen to know where I can find him?"

"I believe he's staying in town," she said with a shrug. "He said he has friends with the local police. But he has been around much. You will see him, I am sure."

She looked down at the list, adding those names to the one she'd compiled. Now, there were only a few missing names, but there it was—a lot of suspects. Where to begin?

"Thank you," she said, standing and heading for the door.

Adila sucked in a breath. "Where are you going?"

She pointed to the door. "I was planning to—"

"You should wait for Mrs. Vandiveer. They are very private people. Would not like you going around without one of them."

Daisy stopped and realized her host, Myrtle, had once again disappeared.

But Myrtle had welcomed her. And if she wanted answers, right away, then . . .

Well, my father always said that, sometimes, you need to break the rules.

Daisy went to the main courtyard and looked around. No Myrtle.

"Oh, well. If you see her, tell her I've gone to take a look at the yacht."

And before Adila could say anything, she stepped into the bright sunshine of mid-morning, hoping she wouldn't get too lost on her way to the marina.

CHAPTER EIGHT

It turned out that all Daisy had to do was follow the sound of the ocean, which led her to a stone terrace overlooking a small, sandy beach enclosed by high cliffs. Next to that, she saw the marina, but from here, it appeared the only way down to it was a long, steep wooden staircase, with multiple switchbacks, clinging rather precariously to the black cliff.

Just looking at it made Daisy feel a little sick. Not only did it give her vertigo—and she'd never had much of a fear of heights—but the thought of climbing *up* the stairs later? She took daily walks and was in reasonably good shape, but such a feat would be daunting to even the hardiest athlete.

I doubt everyone who visits the marina takes these steps. There must be another way back. I'll just find it when I get there, she told herself surely, about to take the first step.

When she grabbed the handle and lowered herself a single step, the entire structure seemed to waver beneath her feet. "This can't be safe," she said aloud, hesitating there.

She looked around and noticed a woman, with a short, white-blonde bob tied up in a handkerchief, sitting on the edge of the terrace in front of a several-stories drop. She was wearing a tight cropped tank and short shorts that bared her tan legs as they dangled over the sharp rocks. But she didn't seem to care that she was just inches from near disaster—she had a professional camera to her eye and was eagerly snapping photographs of the harbor.

Daisy stood there for a moment, watching her, wondering who she was. She was in the confines of the Vandiveer estate, so unless she'd scaled that fence or climbed those stairs from the harbor, she was a guest there. And that meant she was a possible witness. "Hello, there," she called out.

The girl lowered her camera and cocked her head at Daisy, shielding her eyes from the sun. She was young, probably in her early twenties. "Hello yourself. Are you lost?"

"Just looking for a way to get down to the marina."

"Well, those steps will do it for you," she said, scanning the area for her next shot. She lifted her camera to her eye. "It's a bitch, unless you want to take the main road down, but then you'd have to go back to the gate."

She'd known that, of course, there was another way, but she paused, looking at the girl. For someone to know her way around the estate, she had to be close to the Vandiveers. Family. Thinking back to her conversation with Adila, she asked, "Are you Coco?"

She lowered her camera again, her eyes sweeping over Daisy. "Yeah. Who's asking?"

"I'm—"

"Wait. Let me guess. I know. Natasha hired a PI, right?"

Daisy blinked. With those deductive skills, the girl had the makings of a good PI herself. "How did you know?"

She shrugged. "You're American. I knew Natasha was going back to America. And all she talked about after Jacob's death was the injustice of it all." She laughed. "And those shoes look like the type of shoes a PI would wear."

Daisy looked down at her flats. She'd bought them at a discount store, because they were comfortable. And they had been. But if she'd known that she would be coming all the way out to Rhodes and hobnobbing with the obscenely rich, she might've made different fashion choices. "Do you think she's right?"

"Yeah, I guess it is unjust, to her, considering she missed out on the family fortune. She didn't have the nerve to show her face here again after accusing ol' Les of his brother's murder, huh?"

For someone so young, her voice was lower, self-assured. Daisy moved closer. As she did, she noticed the tattoos on the girl's tanned arms. Moons and suns and other celestial objects. She said, "You were there, right? What do you think happened?"

"Well, if it was murder, I don't think Les had anything to do with it," she said, fastening the lens cap onto her camera and letting it fall by the strap onto her chest. "They might not have gotten along, and Jacob might have gotten all the looks in the family, but they were still brothers."

One thing that continually surprised Daisy was that no one seemed particularly sad that Jacob was gone. Even his own mother. She'd thought that it was just the way these wealthy people were, that they were used to being under the microscope and keeping up appearances, but it seemed so strange. Coco, too, didn't look very broken up. "Did you like Jacob?"

"Oh, no. He was such a stuck-up asshole," she said with a laugh. "Vandy, at least, is a real man."

"Vandy?"

"Franklin. His father. He's stuck-up, too, but he has his charm. But I guess all Vandiveers are stuck-up. Me too to a point since they'd rubbed off on me. But at least I'm not some money-obsessed lunatic like the rest of them."

"You're cousins with Lesley . . . how?"

She stared, a little deer-in-headlights for a moment, before saying, "Oh, well now, let's see. My late mother was Vandy's little sister. You've met him, right? One never forgets Vandy, that's for sure."

Daisy thought that it was a little odd that Coco should be so enamored with her uncle, but she nodded along. "But you do think it was murder, then?"

She let out a long breath and turned her pretty, pixie face to the sun. "I don't know. Maybe. Maybe not. All I know is that one day, we were having dinner on the deck of the yacht and Natasha was talking to us about what kind of bridesmaid dresses she wanted us to wear, and the next day, he was dead."

"Did you see any drugs?"

She shook her head. "I don't do drugs. And I don't drink. So I went to bed early that night. And I didn't hear anything because I had my earbuds in. Not that I would have. They were on the master level. There are only two big suites up there, and for some reason, they didn't want to share a room. So, the rest of us were on the next lower level. Right above the servants' quarters."

"Thank you," Daisy said, making a note of this in her book. She hoped that eventually, in addition to a list of suspects, she'd also be able to create a layout of the yacht, pinpointing where everyone was at the time of Jacob's death. Coco's description would help.

"Good luck," Coco muttered, turning toward the house. "With this island of misfit toys, you're going to need it."

But Daisy felt invigorated after the conversation. It felt like she was getting somewhere. She turned to head back down the stairs. For the second time, when she reached the top of the steps, she paused, trying to work up the courage to make the long trip down to the marina. It would be a dangerous descent, but her father always said that the crime scene was where ninety-five percent of the answers could be found.

She had a yacht to explore.

CHAPTER NINE

From the window of her bedroom, Daisy had thought the *Fantasea* was an enormous yacht.

But as she drew closer to it, her jaw dropped. It looked like a cruise ship that was too large for the marina, so it was docked offshore.

She stood there on the long pier, marveling at it. It positively dwarfed the two impressive, million-dollar yachts that were able to fit in the marina. Its chrome fixtures and windows sparkled so blindingly in the sun that Daisy couldn't look directly at it, even when shielding her eyes.

As she was rummaging around in her purse for her sunglasses, a man in white came walking toward her from land. He had a black bag slung over his shoulder, and his shirt was only half-tucked into his pants, exposing his round beer belly. He said something to her in Greek, to which she said, "I'm sorry?"

"Ah, American?" he said with an accent. He pointed to the yacht. "I said she's a beauty, no?"

"I've never seen a yacht this large. How many people can sleep on it?"

"There are thirteen cabins, two on the main owner's deck," he said with a smile. "Over seventy-five meters long. It sleeps twenty-eight guests, twenty-three crew, and four staff."

She raised an eyebrow, impressed. "You know a lot about it."

He grinned at her, his eyes roving over her body as he moved in close. "I should. I've been working on it since Mr. Vandiveer purchased it in 2008. I've been with him for decades, and this little *Fantasea* is his pride and joy. Then again, I suppose it should be, at a price tag of over sixty-three million dollars."

She took a step back. "You're joking."

"No. Not at all. Then again, it's chump change for the Vandiveers. I was surprised when he gifted it to his son, but then again, Mrs. Vandiveer doesn't enjoy sailing."

He'd taken another step closer, and she'd tried to take another step back, but now, she was at the edge of the pier. "Are you a member of the crew?"

"I'm the head chef," he said, extending his hand. "My name is Ramon. And you are lovely. What is your name?"

"Daisy," she said. "I've been hired by the Vandiveers to investigate the murder."

He raised an eyebrow. "Like the other chap?"

Apparently, this Gireau guy had gotten around and made a thorough investigation. "That's right. Have you seen him?"

He nodded. "I think he's on board right now. The yacht has been in port since the murder under the direction of the local police, but we're shipping off again in another few days. I've come to put together my grocery list."

"You're leaving? But if Jacob is gone—"

"The younger Mr. Vandiveer has told me he'd like to go to the Riviera. I think he's had enough. He wants to get away."

Daisy nodded. It was understandable that Lesley would want to get away, considering all the speculation going on outside the gates of the Vandiveer estate. But to leave in the very same vessel where his brother had died? Wasn't that defeating the point of leaving the past behind him?

Ramon put a hand on her arm. "I know. Would you like me to give you a personal tour?" he said with a wink, leaning in so that his warm breath wafted in her face. He smelled like cigar smoke.

As touchy-feely and creepy as this head chef was, she couldn't resist the invitation to see the crime scene up close. "That would be great. But how do you get there?"

"Motorboat, usually. I use a rowboat." He motioned her down the pier, toward the gangplank. As they got into the rowboat, she said, "Where was the destination that night?"

They took off toward the giant ship. "No destination. They just wanted to sail about. We started a few days prior, but we returned to the marina sometime during the early morning."

"Oh." They drew closer, and the ship only got even more enormous, blocking out the sun.

When they reached the ship, she stepped through the corridor into a bright hallway paneled in light wood with chrome fixtures. "This floor," he said, pointing down a corridor, "is the servants' quarters and the kitchen, where I spend most of my time. I'll take you up to the main living areas."

She followed him up a curved staircase with a railing made of chrome and glass. She found herself at the front of the boat. There was a curved, cushioned seating area there as well as a waterfall pool. The deck was pale wood without a blemish or footprint. Daisy imagined that this was probably where Jacob had spent some of his last moments, partying, before his death. "When was the last time you saw Jacob? Was it out here?"

He nodded. "He and the other guests were enjoying some cocktails by the pool before turning in. I usually checked with him to see if I could close the kitchen. He wanted some late-night snacks, so I prepared them for him, handed them off to one of the servants, and then went downstairs to bed."

He led her indoors, past the bridge, to a windowed area with a long dining table, suitable for seating at least twelve guests. There was also a living area, full of pale cream leather couches. She followed him through a hall, past several staterooms, poking her head in each one. "Were all of these occupied?"

"No, as far as parties thrown on this ship, it was a pretty small one. Only a few of these were occupied by members of the wedding party."

"And where was Jacob's room?"

"That's upstairs," he said, pointing. He led her up a short flight of stairs to a lobby with curved walls. There were two doors on either side of her. He motioned to one. "That was where Natasha was staying and . . ."

He went to the other door and opened it.

"Voila. Jacob Vandiveer's room."

She walked in, looking around the semicircle-shaped area. It was very neat and bright, all neutral creams and beiges. Glass and mirrors served to make the space seem even larger. The king bed had an enormous, tufted headboard, and much of the wall was windowed with cream curtains and doors to a balcony. It was spotless; the crime scene had obviously been cleaned.

"Jacob was found over there, in bed," Ramon said, pointing to a spot on the bed near the window.

Daisy nodded. "The housekeeper told me she came to deliver his breakfast and found him there. She said she thought that it was possible he might have been murdered. The coroner's report said a fatal amount of fentanyl had been found in his body. Did you see him using drugs?"

He shook his head slowly. "Not last night at least. I have seen some around. Mostly cocaine, really. I guess it could've been laced with that stuff, right? He just got a bad batch? In which case, it might have been an accident," he said.

"Hmm," she thought, looking around. There was nothing personal in the room at all, nothing to tell her who this Jacob Vandiveer was. "Is that what you think it was?"

"Don't know. I guess it could've been what Natasha said. Murder. But she's a little bit of a lush, so no one really takes what she says seriously."

She turned to look at him and found him lying back on the bed. Very odd, considering it was where a man had died. He was giving her a come-hither look that made her stomach roil as he patted the bed next to him.

"Come sit next to me."

She stared. "Uh, no. What did you mean when you said that Natasha was a lush? She drank a lot?"

"Not all the time. Just morning, noon, and night." He laughed, long and hard, then reached for her hand, holding it tight before she could snatch it away. "So Daisy, where in America are you from?"

She was just about to pull away when the doors to the balcony suddenly slid open.

They both turned as a short man with a goatee came in, eyeing them with disgust. He said something in French, and then mumbled, "Don't mind me," as he strode across the room to the door.

As he opened the door, it occurred to Daisy just who the man was. She snatched her hand away and went after him, dodging around Ramon's outstretched arms as he tried to hold her there. She caught the man as he was about to descend the staircase. "Um, are you Gireau?"

He turned and adjusted his bow tie. He wasn't particularly attractive, and yet he carried himself as though he thought he was, with his chin up and his shoulders back. "*Oui*, I am Gerard Gireau. And who are you?"

"I'm Daisy Fortune," she said, extending her hand for him to shake.

Warily, he reached out and shook just the tips of her fingers, his hand ice cold. Then he opened his notebook and read. "I don't have your name on my list. How do you know me?"

She patted her chest. "I'm also a private detective. I've been looking into the case too."

He inhaled sharply, looking her over. "You are? Who hired you?"

"Well," she began, not sure she should speak about Natasha. "I stopped in and Myrtle Vandiveer said that, although she hired you, two heads would be better than one."

"Oh, she did, did she?" He said, his eyes narrowing. He mumbled something in French, that, from the sharp inflection, Daisy decided wasn't anything nice. "She's a silly woman. I told her that I needed no distractions. And 'another head' is simply a distraction."

She reached into her bag and pulled out her pad. "Oh, but if I—"

"You're an American? What kind of outfit would let someone like you work for them in private investigations?" His words carried the tone of someone who'd just eaten a very unpleasant meal.

Every muscle in her body threatened to shrink down to a miniature size under the weight of this small man's superior glare.

"It's my company, Fortune Investigations. We've actually broken some of the state's largest cases." *Only about forty years ago, but still . . .*

He snorted as if he could sniff right through her lie. "I've solved hundreds of crimes on this island alone. The police and I know every inch of this island, and so when the Vandiveers hired me, I told them that I would happily solve this murder. Not that I would try. That I *would.* It is only a matter of time. And I do not require a sidekick."

Gireau turned to leave, and her jaw dropped. "A sidekick?" she called after him. "I am not a sidekick."

When he spun around, she was surprised to find him laughing at her. Through his smug smile, he said, "You're not mine, anyway."

She frowned at him, then held up her notebook. "I have information in here."

"I'm sure you do. As do I, in my own files. I have detailed profiles on each of the twelve guests and service people who were on board at the time of Jacob Vandiveer's death. But I will not be sharing it with you."

"There's twelve? What about the crew?"

"The crew and the captain are in addition, but—" He stopped. "What do you think you're trying to do?"

"What I was paid to do. By Natasha Blake," she insisted, her chin raised.

"Is that so? Well, Natasha has wasted her money. Because I am already close to coming to a conclusion. So if I were you, I'd pack up my things and go back home." He wiggled his fingers in a wave. *"Au revoir."*

"I'm not going anywhere," she spat out, hands on hips.

His smug smile fell. "All right. In that case, may the best man win."

His dress shoes made a clicking noise as he quickly retreated across the polished wood deck. She stared, frozen, long after he disappeared from sight, her pulse pounding and red-hot anger coursing through her veins.

A moment later, the door to Jacob's room opened, and Ramon appeared. "Now, where were we?"

She held up her palm to him, urging him to come no closer, and stalked down the steps.

Twelve people on board. One was dead, and she'd interviewed a few of the others. But now, she felt like a clock was ticking. She needed to play catch-up so that insufferable jerk of a PI didn't find the answers before she did.

CHAPTER TEN

Twelve.

That number kept running through Daisy's head as she sat on the small beach at the foot of that staircase-from-hell, digging her toes into the sand. She was getting sunburned, but she didn't care.

So much for getting help from Gerard Gireau. Instead, she'd gone and made an archenemy.

Besides, what kind of stupid name was that? Gerard Gireau? And how had he managed to get such a giant head?

She opened her phone and realized that she had at least half a dozen calls and texts from Natasha Blake. The last text was simply a series of question marks. They looked angry.

Quickly, Daisy punched in a call to her. "There you are!" Natasha's dramatic, sing-songy voice came through immediately. "I was worried you'd drowned in the Aegean."

"Sorry. I got a little wrapped up, trying to acclimate myself," she said, feeling proud of what she'd accomplished. Getting access to the estate and the family? It was good progress, considering the plane had touched down only the previous evening. "I've been—"

"Well? Do you know who did it?"

Daisy nearly laughed. She'd made progress, but she wasn't a miracle worker. "No, but I've gotten access to the house, I've spoken to some of the people who had been on board, and I saw the crime sce—"

"Did you talk to him?"

She choked back her words. "Him? Who?"

"Lesley, of course. The killer. Who else?"

"No, I haven't yet. He's—"

"Why not?"

"As I was explaining, when I got up this morning, he'd already gone out golfing with his father," she said. "But I'm planning to talk to him when he gets back. I do think it a little suspicious that he's planning to take the yacht out in a couple of days and go to the Riviera."

"Mmmhmm. Of course. That's because he's the killer. He's been doing all sorts of strange things. He's just been acting very shifty, like he has a lot to hide."

"Okay, well, I'm going to go back to the house and talk to him."

"See that you do."

"Yeah. I wanted to ask you—" She stopped when she realized she was speaking to dead air. "Natasha?"

Nothing. She'd hung up.

Groaning, Daisy navigated to her search engine. She hated disappointing her clients, but now, she wondered if there was any possible way she could actually please someone like Natasha. Or any of the Vandiveers. Other than Myrtle, they all demanded perfection. The servants all seemed to walk on eggshells, afraid of disappointing the "royal" family.

The only hire who didn't seem to think he was unworthy, though? Gerard Gireau.

He clearly thought he was better than most people, just like the Vandiveers. And maybe he was. She typed in the detective's name, only to come up with thousands of search results about cases he'd solved. He hadn't been lying. He was one of Rhodes's premiere detectives, and the police did trust him.

Great. Why did I even bother, she thought, feeling worse.

But then she realized something. He'd made some mistakes. As smart and professional as he was, he had made two mistakes.

First, he'd told her that he didn't, for one moment, think Jacob's death was a suicide or an accident. No. He'd called it a murder.

And second, he'd told her, without a doubt, that there'd been twelve people on board that night.

That made her feel better. Maybe finding the killer wasn't so hopeless. She stared at her list of suspects. She'd already met five of them.

Coco

Natasha

Adila

Milla

Ramon

Minus Jacob, that meant there were six more people who were on board that night. But did it really matter that there were twelve people on board during the night. They'd returned to the marina in the early morning, which meant anyone could have climbed aboard then.

The one person she hadn't yet spoken to, who she knew for sure had been on the yacht, was Lesley. He was her number one suspect, too, at least, according to Natasha. Deciding it was about time to interview him, she stood, brushed the sand off her backside, and began the long climb up to the estate.

She was out of breath before she'd even gone a quarter of the way. Stopping and gasping for air, she saw someone up above her, coming down, taking the stairs at a breakneck pace. It was a tanned man in nothing but dark sunglasses and a tiny red bathing suit.

He cocked his head in her direction as he jogged past. "*Kalimera,*" he said to her, which she assumed was good morning in Greek, since he'd been smiling.

"Same to you," she responded, between huffs of air.

By the time she reached the top of the staircase, the man in the red suit was doing laps in the blue sea. A she watched him, wondering who he was, a hand reached out and grabbed her arm.

Stunned, she whirled to find Adila there. "Miss," she said, breathless. "You must come with me."

"What is the problem?"

Her cheeks were flushed as if she'd been recently running in a long race. "Mr. Vandiveer came back from his golf trip and found out you were on the grounds without an escort. He's cross."

"At me? Really?"

Adila wrung her hands. "Yes. Please. Do not delay."

"Okay. You think he's going to kick me out?"

She nodded without hesitation.

"Really? He's that much of a monster?"

She nodded again and turned to rush toward the main house.

Daisy broke into a run hurrying after the skinny maid, who was walking at such a clip that she might as well have been flying. "But Myrtle didn't seem to mind that—"

"Yes, but Mr. Vandiveer is the man of the house."

Daisy's mind flashed with images of being kicked out of the compound again. And she hadn't even interviewed the main suspect, Lesley. "Well, even if it's not a democracy, she gets a vote, doesn't she? What are the chances the son will be reasonable and see it my way too?"

Adila stopped and looked at Daisy as if she had three heads. "Mr. Lesley? Oh, no. He is even worse than his father."

She winced, surprised. She hadn't heard that about the younger Vandiveer son. She'd had it in her mind that Jacob was the brash, confident one, blessed with good looks, and Lesley was the shy, backward son, who was used to blending into the scenery. Maybe Natasha was right when she pinpointed him as the killer.

When she reached the door to the living area, she heard voices coming from inside, raised in anger. She took a deep breath and followed Adila inside.

Before Adila could properly announce Daisy's presence, the elder Vandiveer swung around and jabbed a finger at Daisy. "There you are! What's the meaning of this? You're not to go anywhere without an escort! I'm sure that was made clear to you."

Myrtle sat on the edge of the high-backed chair, looking scolded, as if her husband had been yelling directly at her. "It might have slipped my mind, dear," she said quietly.

Daisy's eyes were drawn to a young man, who must've been in his mid-twenties, who was sulking on the sofa like a teenager. He had dark, floppy hair, and looked a bit like Jacob, with that same smug, superior expression. He studied his fingernails, bored. "Of course Mom forgot. The bottom line is that we don't need strangers traipsing around here. That's what the giant fence is for."

When he finally looked up, his blue eyes caught hers in an accusing glare.

She cleared her throat. "Yes, I understand. But I was just trying to do my job."

Lesley rolled his eyes. "But your name isn't Gireau. We hired Gerard Gireau to handle all this, didn't we, Mom?"

Myrtle looked over at him. "*You* didn't hire anyone. And I only thought having more people looking into it would only help us arrive at the truth sooner."

"Yes, dear," Mr. Vandiveer said, shaking his head. "But it's dangerous. You know that. And we already know what happened. It was an accident."

Lesley nodded along. "Yeah. Dad's right."

Of course, he would think that if he was the killer. He wouldn't want anyone investigating at all.

For a moment, Daisy thought the mild-mannered, sweet Southern lady would let her husband steamroll over her, the way he seemed to do to all the help. But then Myrtle cleared her throat and stood up. "Sweetheart," Myrtle said to her husband. "The coroner's report suggested a suicide. That he took that awful drug on purpose. And I don't believe that for a second. There is nothing wrong with asking questions, just to make sure. That report damages his good name. And I won't have it."

Both male Vandiveers stared at her for a long time. Franklin went to the fireplace and rested his elbow on the mantle. Then he let out a sigh. "Fine. But we only need Gireau. There are too many hands meddling in this. You know—"

"I don't like Gireau. He's oily and smug," she announced, glancing at Daisy. "I like Daisy. An American. She's already making so much headway, running all over this compound. Aren't you, dear?"

Daisy nodded. "Yes. I was at the crime scene, and—"

"Our private yacht," Vandiveer grumbled with a sigh. "Poking through our private things. I don't like it. She's a stranger."

"I don't like not knowing about our poor Jacob," Myrtle said with a final nod. "And if it makes you feel better, I'll keep a close eye on her. But I insist that she investigate."

Both male Vandiveers eventually nodded, giving in. "Fine," Mr. Vandiveer said, his jaw tight. "I still think it's a bad idea. So if I have any indication that anyone is being harassed or threatened by this woman, I'm going to call the police. You get that?"

Daisy swallowed, sufficiently worried.

"Oh, don't worry about him," Myrtle whispered to her, smiling. "I'm sure you have some questions to ask Lesley, don't you?"

Daisy nodded. "Yes, please. If you wouldn't mind."

The younger Vandiveer morphed into the sullen, sulky teenager again. Hands curled into fists, he sneered at his mother.

"I've got to move my car," he said and stalked out of the house.

"I apologize. He's been wrecked since the death of his beloved brother. They were always the best of friends. I suppose you'll have to speak with him later," Myrtle said with a shrug. "Can I have the ladies bring you some tea?"

Personally, Daisy was all tea-ed out. She wanted to make things happen. She'd let Lesley Vandiveer go for now, but he couldn't avoid her forever. “Jacob had a room in the house, yes? Would you mind showing me around there?”

“Absolutely. Adila can show you right up.” She looked at her husband and added, “And if you wouldn’t mind staying with her, I’d appreciate it.”

Daisy nodded. “Of course,” she said, but she wondered why Mr. Vandiveer was so eager to keep an eye on her and didn’t want her poking around. Did he just like his privacy? Or was there some deep, dark family secret he was hiding?

CHAPTER ELEVEN

As Adila took her up the curved staircase to the second floor, Daisy hung back, peering in different rooms, hoping for some clue as to how this family worked. As far as she knew, a couple things were clear—one, that they wanted their privacy, and two, that most of them did not appreciate her intruding upon it. Why that was and whether it had to do with Jacob's death still remained to be seen.

There was also the matter of the treatment of the servants. She definitely had the feeling that none of them were happy with their employers. They seemed appreciative to have the job, but there was no love lost with the Vandiveers. The only person the servants seemed to like was Myrtle. So not only did that make all the servants suspects, but it also made it possible that they'd be eager to condemn a member of the family for the murder.

"Who do these rooms belong to?" Daisy asked as they went past the first two. The hallway was arched and airy, and a cool ocean breeze wafted through the white arched walls, making it comfortable and pleasant. Though she tried to take her time, she only caught a glimpse of each room before Adila turned back to her, urging her to hurry with a severe glance.

She shrugged. "No one. Most rooms in here belong to no one. They are just empty rooms."

Empty rooms, and yet each seemed bright and cheery and filled with nice furniture. "They have lots of guests, then."

"Yes, they do. Mrs. Vandiveer loves to entertain."

She passed one with a bunch of art easels, and a rather rudimentary painting of the sea, drying in one corner.

Before she could ask the question, Adila said, "Mrs. Vandiveer is an artist."

"Oh," Daisy said, motioning to the painting. "That's very good."

"Hmm," Adila said, clearly disagreeing. Daisy had said it just to be nice, but Adila didn't strike her as a person who said things to spare people's feelings. She stepped on, her movements tight and efficient.

As Daisy followed, she noticed that Adila sped up to pass the door of one room. The door was partially closed, but it made her curious. Was there something inside that Adila did not want her to see?

When she went past it, she saw an electric guitar propped on a stand in the corner. Nothing else, but it intrigued her. Everything else in the place was standard and impersonal like a hotel lobby. It said nothing about the home's occupants. The guitar was the first personal thing she'd seen.

She couldn't imagine someone like Myrtle or Franklin Vandiveer owning such a thing. So did that mean this was Lesley's room?

As she inched closer, Adila cleared her throat.

She looked up. Adila pointed down the hallway. Situated high among the cliffs, it appeared to open up on one side to a view of the ocean below. "This way."

Daisy hastened her step until she was at the overlook. It was as if whoever designed the home knew that the most breathtaking views were right at this spot and had decided to make good use of it. She found herself on a walkway to another wing of the house. Down below her was the sea, and that beach she'd been to earlier. Up this high, she had a panoramic view of the sea, from the cliffs to her left to the marina on her right.

This time, Adila didn't seem to mind her hesitating. Likely, everyone did. "It is lovely, no?"

She nodded.

"Jacob Vandiveer's room is right this way."

At the very next door, Adila stepped aside and presented it to her. She went in, immediately dazzled by the view from the balcony outside. It was so captivating that she almost forgot what she'd come for. When she did finally tear her gaze away from the sea, she was disappointed. Impersonal, just like a hotel room.

She inched over to a drawer and opened it, peering inside. It was empty. "Did the Vandiveers have this room cleaned out?"

Adila nodded. "Mr. Vandiveer asked us to."

Well, of course, now it made sense why Mr. Vandiveer hadn't complained when she'd asked to come up here. They already knew that she'd find nothing. If the Vandiveers wanted her to solve this case, this wasn't the way to go about it.

And maybe they didn't? What secrets were they hiding?

At that moment, Daisy made a decision. If she was going to solve this case, she was going to have to go where she wasn't allowed.

She poked around a little more, then went out to the balcony overlooking the ocean. From there, the top of the majestic *Fantasea*, docked in the marina, was just visible. She turned to find Adila watching her carefully. "Is there anything else I can show you, Miss?"

Daisy shook her head, gathering her courage as she followed the maid outside. As they went past the room with the guitar, she felt the familiar curious itch that was typical of the Fortune family. She desperately wanted to see what was on the other side.

Of course, Adila just kept going, and Daisy had no choice but to follow.

But just as they reached the top of the steps, two things happened. Daisy noticed a restroom, and Mrs. Vandiveer called up from the courtyard. "Adila! We're having games on the terrace. And perhaps our guest would want an Ouzito?"

Daisy stared at Adila in confusion.

Adila whispered, "It is one of Mr. Vandiveer's specialty cocktails."

"Oh," Daisy said with a nod. Even though the male Vandiveers clearly didn't like her, at least she was being invited to their social functions. It would be a good opportunity to learn more about them. However, she got the feeling the main reason for inviting her was to keep her close, so she couldn't let her eyes wander.

"Adila! Can you help serve?" Myrtle Vandiveer called.

Adila quickly took the first two steps. Daisy glanced back down the hall toward the room she'd wanted to investigate. She pointed toward the restroom. "Actually, mind if I use the facilities?"

Adila's face turned wary, but she nodded. "I suppose. The terrace is out back. Please do not be long. The Vandiveers don't like to be kept waiting."

"Oh, I won't," she said with a smile, going in and closing the door without twisting the lock. She waited a few beats, and when she heard Adila's footfalls reach the bottom of the staircase, she slowly opened the door. Then she crept back down the hall, away from the stairs, acutely aware of every noise her shoes made on the tile floor.

When she reached the solid wooden door, she pushed it open carefully, afraid that it would creak and give her away. But it made no sound as she slowly pushed it, and what it revealed was instantly promising.

It was more interesting than possibly anything else in the museum of a mansion. The rest of the house had been equipped with carefully curated objects meant to convey beauty and opulence. But this room was like the dirty little secret of the house, the place they wished to keep behind locked doors. Daisy knew that the second she peered in as she saw the room was an absolute mess, strewn with papers and laundry and garbage on every surface.

Now, I might get somewhere, she thought, forgetting to be quiet as she moved across the room, navigating around the piles of discarded clothes. As she reached a desk covered in a small mountain of papers, the floorboards beneath her feet creaked.

She winced, then looked back toward the door, listening for steps on the staircase outside.

Hearing nothing, she started to page through the paper. A lot of it was junk mail: invitations for certain investing schemes, advertisement from different investors, a letter from the alumni association of his prestigious alma mater in America, soliciting donations. There were even a few euros scattered among the pile, and one note for 500 euros was cast aside like it was a candy wrapper. But it wasn't that which held her attention. What did was a letter addressed to an attorney in America, James Willard Prescott, Esq, from the younger Vandiveer brother.

She lifted the letter and noted the date, from two weeks prior to Jacob's death. It read:

Mr. Prescott,

You are one of my father's closest advisors, and I know you won't understand this, but I ask you not to question my reasoning as I've thought long and hard about it.

I would like to disclaim my interest in Vandiveer Holdings as soon as feasible. I understand that upon my father's death, the business would be split between us, but I don't want it. I've chosen to forge my own path and I'm—

"What are you doing?"

Daisy looked up to see Lesley Vandiveer, standing in the doorway, staring at her with his eyes, narrowed in rage.

CHAPTER TWELVE

Daisy froze, feeling her face turn as red as a sunset.

In her past investigations, she'd been caught with her hand in the cookie jar a handful of times, and she'd managed to artfully explain her way out of it.

"I, uh . . ." She looked around for an excuse. Nothing came. Every excuse that hit her mind seemed silly. There was no hope of fudging her way out of this. "I was just investigating—"

"You were going through my things, invading my privacy!" he snapped, striding across the room and snatching the letter from her hand. He glanced at it and shook his head, then folded it and stuffed it under the mountain.

"What was that?" she asked quietly, aware that any false move could rock the boat she was teetering on. "You didn't want Vandiveer Holdings?"

He stared at her for a moment, as if trying to determine whether he should bother answering. Then he exhaled. "Yes. I've never wanted any part in my father's empire." He motioned to his guitar. "My music business is really taking off. I have fans in Thailand now."

"Oh," she said, raising her eyebrows to give him the illusion that she was impressed. "But if you disclaimed the business, who would it go to?"

He shrugged. "My brother was supposed to have full control. And then, the hope was that when he had kids, they'd take over. I wanted no part in it. But with him gone, if I renounced, upon my father's death, the business would be broken up and sold to the highest bidders. I might be an idiot who just wanted to tour the world with my guitar, but I can't let that happen. My mother would be heartbroken."

"So, you are here for duty."

He sat on the edge of his unmade bed and raked his fingers through his hair. "Yeah. I guess I am."

If that was true, and the letter seemed to confirm it, then contrary to what Natasha thought, Lesley had no business murdering his brother. "But you were on the *Fantasea* on the night your brother died, right?"

He nodded. "And I'm sure you think I'm suspect number one because you heard we had an argument. Right?"

She blinked. "Actually, I never heard that. You had an argument? About what?"

He sighed and shook his head. "It was the same old thing we always argued about. He wanted me to stay and be his right-hand man in the business. He thought my music career was a waste of time. He never understood it."

"When did you fight?"

"I don't know. Right after dinner. He kept throwing digs at me while we were on deck, so I ordered the captain to take us to shore. I got off the boat and went to the beach to collect myself."

"How long were you on the beach?"

"'Til morning."

"Morning?"

He nodded. "I was drunk. I slept on the beach. I sobered up, and when I went back to give him a piece of my mind, it was morning. I was just getting back on the ship when I heard the commotion. People were saying that something was wrong with Jacob."

"You were alone when you got off the ship? On the beach?"

He shook his head. "I was with Rose and Maureen."

"Rose and Maureen?"

"Yeah. Rose is Natasha's best friend since birth, and Maureen's her college roommate, I think? I don't know. I just met them that night. They were on the yacht too. The whole wedding party was there, but I didn't know most of them."

Daisy's mouth made an O. She'd forgo questioning exactly what the three of them were doing on the beach. But those were two more of the twelve she could cross off her list of suspects. "Most of the wedding party were Americans?"

He nodded. "Yeah."

"They all went home, I'm assuming? No sense staying around."

"I don't know about Rose. But Maureen was staying the month at the Hotel Rodos. Her father owns the place as well as half the island."

Of course. That was where Natasha was staying too. "You have any idea who could've done this to your brother?"

"Like I said, I don't think anyone did. I think he overdosed. Maybe intentionally. He was under a lot of stress, getting ready to assume the business, marry the perfect girl . . . he came across like he had nerves of steel, like nothing ever rattled him. Typical firstborn. But I think it might've been too much." He leaned forward and stared at the ground. "And after our fight . . . I think maybe it was my fault."

"Your fault? Why?"

He looked at her like she was insane. "Because I told him that I didn't want the business. I abandoned him. Maybe it was too much."

"So you think he took the fentanyl intentionally?"

He shrugged. "Can't imagine that anyone else on board would've slipped it to him."

"But you just said that you didn't know them?"

His nose wrinkled, like he couldn't recall, then he burst out in sour laughter. "All right, so I did. But no one had a reason to as far as I could see. Those were all his friends on board, the people he trusted most. Who'd do that? Unless it was one of the staff."

"Or unless someone else came on board when the yacht was at port."

He frowned. "Oh. Yeah. I guess that's true."

"There's no security camera on board or in the marina?"

He shook his head. "Nope."

Sure, all the money in the world, and yet not enough to spend a lousy $100 on a video camera, she thought, thinking of her dingy little apartment in East Plainfield. That place had security cameras all over. But then again, this was paradise. And nothing bad ever happened here.

Whoever had committed the murder likely knew that there was no security in place on the ship. But that could've been anyone.

One thing seemed pretty obvious, though—the killer wasn't Lesley Vandiveer. Which meant that Natasha's guess was all wrong.

And, it brought her, with a sinking feeling, back to square one.

Before she could ask another question, Myrtle appeared in the doorway. "Oh, there you are!" she said brightly. "I was worried you were alone, but if you're with Lesley, here, everything's all right. Making friends?"

Lesley grunted as Myrtle's eyes went around the room, narrowing in disgust at its unkempt state.

Daisy smiled. "Yes, we were just chatting."

"Well, come on downstairs to the terrace. It's much better than this stinky, stuffy disaster," she said, ushering them out. "You have to try one of Mr. Vandiveer's famous Ouzitos!"

Daisy nodded. "Sure."

She'd spend a few moments on the terrace to be kind to her hosts. But now, she knew she needed to get to the Hotel Rodos and speak to Maureen and—most importantly, Natasha—as soon as possible.

CHAPTER THIRTEEN

Daisy finally escaped the terrace get-together in the late afternoon.

It wasn't her scene, at all. She'd expected something simple, last-minute, but this event had been clearly well-planned. There were a number of wealthy people from about the island in brightly-colored island garb, all talking about expensive items they'd bought, extravagant trips they'd taken, or important people they knew. There was a Greek band playing love songs and expensive hors d'oeurvres dispensed from gleaming silver dishes. Daisy had navigated around the room, trying to find anyone who might have been present when Jacob died, but she had a hard time breaking into their tight circles and carrying on conversation when she had nothing to add.

Girard Gireau, though? He'd been there and had melted expertly into the crowd as if he was one of them. Maybe he was. Every so often, he'd give her sneering, superior looks. Eventually, she'd wound up sitting by the bar, shoveling *spanakopitas* into her mouth and drinking far too much.

Girard Gireau is definitely going to solve this case before I do, she thought miserably, sipping her drink.

Then she scolded herself. That was no way to think. If he were here, her father would've told her to man up. That was what he'd always said, even when she was a little girl. It had always just been the two of them, and even then, Daisy couldn't imagine anything better than growing up to be just like her father.

Man up, Daisy, she told herself, squaring her shoulders and setting the empty drink down on a tray. She refused to give up this early.

As she navigated her way to the front gate of the Vandiveer estate to wait for her cab to the Hotel Rodos on the other side of the island, she was more than a little tipsy. She'd only had three of the drinks, which were similar to Mojitos, but she wasn't used to the alcohol, so everything in her vision seemed to waver.

As she waited, she called Natasha, who once more jumped on her with an, "Any news?"

"Yes, actually," she said, leaning against a wall. Her vision was starting to spin, and for a moment, she wondered if someone had poisoned *her* drink. "But I'm coming there to see you."

"All right, darling," her wealthy employer said, once again ending the call without any formal goodbyes.

She pocketed her phone and blinked, trying to focus on the palm trees in the dying light of day. *Did* someone put something in her drink so that she wouldn't be able to find the truth about what happened? Or was she really that much of a lightweight? She tried to remember when she'd last had an alcoholic beverage, but couldn't.

Don't overreact, Daisy. You've simply come a long way from your college days.

When she got in the cab, she tried to think about how to break the news of Lesley's innocence to Natasha. She'd have to do it delicately, because she already knew that Natasha was a drama queen and would overreact to even the slightest bit of bad news. She leaned her head against the window and yawned.

The next thing she knew, the cab driver was barking something at her in Greek. Blinking, she raised her head and found that she'd been drooling. Again.

She looked out the window and saw the most magnificent, castle-like hotel, made of bright pink sandstone. HOTEL RODOS was written above the giant arched doorway in elegant script.

"Oh, I'm here," she said drowsily, realizing that was probably what the driver was trying to tell her. She reached into her purse, swiped her credit card, and stepped out. Before she could turn to thank the driver, he sped off, making her wonder how long she'd been dozing in the back seat.

Even in her sensible shoes, she tottered to the curb. A few valets watched her like she was a time bomb about to go off, and one asked if she needed assistance. She waved him off and went through the doors into the opulent lobby.

Her jaw dropped as she gazed up to the stained-glass artwork on the ceiling, and she almost lost her balance. Grabbing her phone, she propped herself up against a sturdy column and dialed Natasha's number. "I'm here at the hotel," she said when Natasha answered.

"Oh, perfect, darling," she said, every syllable drawn out with dramatic flair. "We're out catching the last rays of sun. You come on over poolside, and we can catch up then."

Once again, call ended.

Daisy scanned the place, looking for a sign pointing the way to the pool. Instead, she saw a man in a red jacket and brass nameplate, smiling at her. Actually, two men. Twins.

Only one voice said, in an echo chamber, "May I help you?"

It hit her, as her gut began to churn, that what she was seeing wasn't right. Her eyes were deceiving her. Blinking to try to pull the dual image into one, she pressed herself against the column. When she opened her eyes, it hadn't done any good. She spoke directly between them. "Pool?"

He pointed the way, toward a hall and a set of double doors. He also said more, something about providing assistance, but Daisy only heard fragments. She made her way to back doors, vaguely aware that she was staggering by the way everyone around her seemed to stare and step away from her, as if they were afraid of catching whatever disease she had.

When she reached the pool, she paused at the door handle, trying to get her bearings. Stepping outside, she hoped the sun and ocean air would help, but as she looked around the vast oasis of a pool area, she felt worse.

She scanned the cabanas and lounge chairs, looking for the stunning, raven-haired beauty, and found her immediately. Natasha was a standout among people who were used to standing out. She was sitting up in her lounge chair, in a barely-there black bikini that showed off her toned figure, a floppy hat and dark sunglasses covering her face. But Daisy could tell that it was her, even tipsy and with the edges of her vision blurring.

As Daisy approached, she noticed a tan woman lying flat on her stomach next to her. She'd untied the back straps on her own bikini so that her entire back was bare, and seemed to be asleep.

"Darling," she said as Daisy stood in front of her.

Daisy waved. "H—"

"Stop blocking my sun, for goodness's sake. Sit down, sit down," she mumbled, exasperated, pointing to the empty lounge chair next to her. "You look like you're about to fall down. What have you been up to?"

True to Natasha's prediction, Daisy practically fell into the chair next to her. "I had a few Ouzitos and—"

"Oh, that explains it. Those are not for those with weak constitutions, right, Mo?"

A muffled "yes" came from the woman next to her. Daisy wasn't sure she liked being pegged as having a weak constitution, but she had more important things on her mind. Since Natasha wasn't making introductions, she said, "Are you Maureen?"

She cracked an eye open. "Who's asking?"

"Mo, this is Daisy. She's the PI I told you I brought from the states."

Maureen propped herself up on her elbows, giving Daisy a thorough eye-raking, stopping at her shoes.

That's it. I am getting new shoes the second I find a store.

"Oh, right. Nice to meet you. I bet you have questions for me."

Daisy nodded. Maybe Gireau hadn't gotten around to questioning her yet. *Oh, who am I kidding? Gireau has probably interviewed everyone.* "You're Natasha's college roommate? You were with Lesley the night of the murder."

Maureen gritted her teeth and looked at her friend. "Don't remind me."

Natasha's jaw went wide. "What?"

"It was a huge mistake. But we were all pretty smashed." Then she glared at Daisy. "Thanks for telling her."

Natasha let out a little yelp. "Mo, darling. You listened to me blather on incessantly about how I was certain Lesley had killed Jacob. And all this time, you knew it wasn't him?"

"Well . . ." She shrugged. "I mean, he could've. Lesley could've poisoned his drink before we left the yacht."

Daisy shook her head. "It's not that he didn't have the opportunity. The fact is that he isn't interested at all in the business. He wanted to pursue his music career. He really had no reason to kill Jacob."

"Oh, *puhleeze*," Natasha said, waving a manicured hand at her as she sipped her frozen drink. "That's ludicrous. Of course he wanted the business. Why would you ever think otherwise? It's worth millions upon millions!"

"Not only did he come across as sincere when I spoke to him, but I found a letter he'd planned to send his attorney, detailing his plans to forfeit his stake in the family business," Daisy said, leaning against the back of the chair, since her head was now starting to spin.

"Probably forged," Natasha said.

"No, actually," Maureen piped up. "I spent a long time speaking to him about it, too, that night on the beach. He kept saying that he knew it would upset Jacob, but his heart wasn't in it. He really wanted to make a go of his band."

Natasha rolled her eyes. "Ridiculous. That band of his sounds worse than a flock of wounded seagulls."

Maureen shrugged and looked at Daisy. "Still . . ."

"I think we need to look elsewhere to find the killer, assuming that it was a murder. Lesley seemed to think it might be suicide, and Mr. Vandiveer seems to concur."

She flicked a bug from her forearm. "Absolutely not. Jacob wouldn't do that. I knew him best. He was murdered." She reached out and grabbed Daisy's arm suddenly. "Please. Find the killer. You must. I can't tell you—"

She lowered her head, and for a moment, Daisy thought she might see a glimpse of actual emotion from her.

"—I can't tell you how many sleepless nights I've had, wondering," she said, her voice cracking. "It's been terrible."

"I understand. I'll try." Daisy went to put a hand atop Natasha's hand, which was resting on her arm, as a gesture of comfort.

But before she could, Natasha moved away and flicked her off like the bug that had been on her forearm. Her voice turned hard again. "If that's all, I'll let you get back to it."

Then she turned away, as if Daisy was one of her servants.

And in a way, that was all she was.

So, Daisy let out a sigh, shuffled out of the chair, and rose to her feet. But as she sat up, something occurred to her. "Oh," she began. "One more thing."

Natasha looked at her, annoyed. "You're in my sun again."

Daisy moved to the side, but that only seemed to make her shadow bigger. She moved to the other side, but the sudden movement made her head feel like it was two feet thick. She grabbed the side of her face, massaging her temple.

"Yes?" Natasha prompted, her lips pursed tight.

"I have about half the people who were on the boat that night, and I've cleared them. But do you think you can give me the names of any . . ." She stopped, as a strange feeling started to come over her. She felt like her legs were no longer her own, like she was just floating there. "Any . . ."

“Any what?” she heard Natasha say, but Daisy couldn’t quite see anymore, because vision swirled. She didn’t see double anymore. She saw all colors, mixing together like a child’s fingerpainting.

“The names of the people . . .” Was she talking? She wasn’t just thinking, was she? Why did her tongue feel so misshapen, hard and useless, like a tree trunk in her mouth? She tried again. “The names of the people on the yacht with . . .”

She trailed off, and before she knew it, the pink pavers that had once been under her feet began rising up to meet her, and she could do nothing to stop it.

And then the world faded to black.

CHAPTER FOURTEEN

Daisy woke to find herself in a lush cabana, surrounded by swaying, gauzy curtains. The cushions beneath her were soft and luxurious, and she sank comfortably into them tasting the sweet ocean air. All she needed was a fruity tropical drink and a sweet, understanding man to share it all with, and it would be perfect.

"This is heaven," she whispered. Exactly the vacation she'd always dreamed of having—her, in some paradise, with nothing to do but relax.

But then she realized that she'd never made any reservations. Hadn't gone to the airport. Hadn't even packed for a trip to the islands. In fact, she'd been working a case, not very long ago. And . . . what had happened with it?

She cracked an eye open and realized that she wasn't wearing a bathing suit. Not even close; she was wearing a professional blouse and blazer, the exact thing she usually wore when following a case, though now, it was quite a bit more rumpled than she was used to. And . . . was that dirt on the front of it?

Then she rolled over and saw a number of servants in red jackets, staring at her with concern. One of them was fanning her face with his hand.

"Are you all right, ma'am?" a woman said, lifting a bottle to her lips.

Embarrassed, she tried to sit up to drink, but her head still spun. As she sipped the cold water, she looked around for her employer. "Natasha?"

The woman shook her head. "Ms. Blake had to go back to her room, regretfully. She had dinner reservations. She asked us to see to you. An ambulance is on its way."

"Oh," Daisy said, not sure why she felt disappointed. Of course, Natasha wasn't her friend. She couldn't think any more, though, because her head ached. "No need for an ambulance. I'm fine. Just passed out from the heat."

Of course, it wasn't. It was those damn drinks. And while she'd have loved to blame it on someone poisoning her to stop her from solving the case, it was likely she'd just drunk too much. She needed to be careful and smarter, this time. She was approaching her second day in Rhodes, and she was no closer to finding out the truth. She needed to get moving.

Gingerly, she slid to the edge of the bed, still clutching the side of her head. "Thank you, everyone. I've got to go . . ."

"Oh. Take this, ma'am," the woman said, handing her the bottle of water and a piece of paper. "Ms. Blake said that it was for you."

She unfolded it to find a list of names. The twelve who'd been aboard. She knew half of them, but the others, who she assumed were either servants or members of the bridal party, she hadn't heard of before. If Natasha had been here, she would've asked her to clarify. But right now, they were just names—some, only half-names, like *Faye.*

But at least it was a start. She stood up, clinging to the cabana's vertical column for support, then slowly made her way back to the hotel. "Thank you so much."

The walk across the grand hotel lobby seemed to take an eternity, but by the time she reached transportation services and asked for a cab, she felt a little better. She got into the cab, staring at the list, and called Natasha again.

"Oh, you're alive, darling," she said without sounding relieved at all. "Sorry I had to leave you, but Mo made reservations months ago for an exclusive place on the beach, and she simply would've killed me if we missed."

Daisy wasn't sure about that. Since Maureen's family owned half the island, she was pretty sure they could've gone wherever they wanted, whenever they wanted to. But she shrugged. "I'm fine. Thanks for the list. Can I ask you who these people are?"

She sighed. "All of them? I thought a good detective might know off the bat?"

"I've met more than half of them. But who is Zachary Hardy? No one has mentioned him?"

"Oh, him," she said, and Daisy could almost hear her rolling her eyes on the other end. "He's a loathsome attorney. One of Jacob's friends."

"In the wedding party?"

"No . . ." she said, pausing as if some great thought had occurred to her. "That's funny. I don't really know why he was there. I didn't even think he was that good a friend of Jacob's, to be honest."

"Okay," Daisy said, scanning the list. "And this person, Miranda Castleton. Is she a friend of yours, in the bridal party?"

"Friend of Jacob's family. I don't know much about her," she said shortly, dismissively. "Look. I've got to go. Our table is ready."

She wanted to ask about the other names, but the cab was pulling up at the Vandiveer estate, and she had enough to go on for now. Daisy said, "Okay, well, I'm going to look into this tonight and then I'll—"

She stopped when she realized that she was talking to dead air.

Groaning, she shoved her phone in her pocket, wondering if she would ever learn. To people like Natasha Blake and most of the rich and important, a second-rate detective didn't matter at all.

But maybe that was a good thing. If they thought she didn't matter, maybe they'd forget she was there, drop their airs, and tell the truth. She could only hope.

This time, she made it through the front gate with only a mild grilling. Apparently, Myrtle had thought to add her to the relatively short guest list. As she was walking around the main fountain outside the circular drive, she saw someone standing on the rim of the fountain, silhouetted by the fading sun.

"Stay right there!"

Daisy froze, wondering if she was about to get in trouble again, when there was the click of a camera shutter, and the figure jumped down into her vision. It was Coco, the Vandiveer's cousin, staring at her handiwork. "Got that. Looks perfect."

Daisy looked over at the camera's latest shot and grimaced. She'd gotten Daisy from an extremely high angle, so all that really showed was her confusion-wrinkled brow and her "PI shoes." She mumbled, "What are you going to call that? Private Eye in Turmoil?"

"Are you?" Coco asked, head tilted. "So, I take it the investigations aren't going so swimmingly?"

"Dead in the water," she muttered, unfolding the paper Natasha had given her. "You wouldn't happen to know where I could find some of these people?"

"Oh, is this a list of the other pretentious kids at that party?" she asked scanning the list. "Who did you get this from?"

"Natasha. Myrtle said there are no other guests staying on property, so I'm assuming they're no longer here, but—"

"No, they are. That's the thing about these people. They have an abundance of leisure time. They never rush anywhere." She grinned. "They might not be staying at the property, but they're around. I think this girl—Miranda—came by her own yacht. She's probably still docked at the marina."

"Really?"

"Yeah, but I don't think she would have anything to do with it."

"Why is that?"

"Well, she was probably younger than me, even, and she never talked to Jacob at all. She just sat there in the back. She and Natasha were giving each other looks the whole time, but I don't think I heard her say one word to anyone."

"But I thought Natasha said that she was Jacob's friend?"

Coco shrugged. "Didn't look like it. And let's see . . . this guy? Zachary? He must've been the squirrely looking, uptight guy in the corner. I think I heard he was Vandy's attorney's son." She gasped. "Come to think of it, he was really weird. He didn't really talk to anyone the whole time, either. Just kind of sat back and observed, like he was waiting for the right time to strike. It could've been him, you know. I actually saw him near the stairs to Jacob's room before I went to bed."

"You did?"

She nodded. "I don't know why I didn't think of that until just now. He was perspiring something awful." She laughed. "He was so wet, I thought he'd fallen overboard. I remember him, with a handkerchief, wiping his forehead, but it didn't help. He was sweating like pig."

"Do you know where I could find him?"

"Well, let me see. The offices of Hardy and Hardy are on the mainland," Coco said. "Vandy talks about it all the time."

Daisy sighed. A trip to the mainland would take all day. "That's the firm he works for? I'll have to phone him, then."

"Yep, like I said, he's in it with his dad, but I think he's been taking over more and more because his father's old. But not so fast. From what I hear, he has clients all over the island, so he's here more than he's in the office, since his father is too old to make the trip. I don't know how anyone could trust him, but his father was very well respected. When Vandy told everyone to clear out after Jacob died because they wanted their privacy, I think Zachary went to stay with the Lafayettes." She jumped back on the rim of the fountain and stood on her tip toes, searching for something. Then she grabbed for Daisy's hand. "Come up here."

"What? Why?" she said as Coco gripped her hand tightly and hoisted her up.

"I'm showing you. Look. You see that tower there?"

Daisy had to stand on her toes, too, but she could just make out an old belltower, among the high palms. It wasn't far in the distance, maybe a mile away. "What about it?"

"That's where the Lafayettes live. You could probably walk it if you wanted."

She did. Now, she felt like she had a fully formed plan of attack. Zachary first, and then Miranda Castleton on the yacht. Even though it felt like Girard was way ahead of her, it was something. "Thanks."

"As for the other names," Coco said, scanning the list. "Can't help you. *Milla?* I don't know who that is. I'm not good with names."

"Well, Milla's a maid. I met her yesterday," Daisy said, happy she'd made some progress. "But the other, I have no idea. Guess I'll keep digging."

She jumped from the fountain, and something came to her. "Actually, one more question. You spoke to Gireau, right?"

She nodded.

"Did he ask you about Zachary?"

"Nope. I mean, the Hardy family is the first name that comes to mind when people in Rhodes are looking for an attorney, and Gireau is the first person they think of when it comes to private investigations. They must be friendly. I got the feeling Gireau already knew everything about him."

Maybe he did. Maybe he knew Zachary Hardy so well—or thought he did—that he skipped right over him. But what he didn't know, and what Coco just remembered, was that he'd been standing outside Jacob's stateroom, perspiring heavily, shortly before the murder.

It wasn't a lot. But it was one thing she had over Gireau. Maybe he knew these people *too well,* and wouldn't suspect anyone, especially people who had connections that could destroy his career if he laid blame in the wrong place. He would do everything possible not to step on their toes. But Daisy didn't have that problem. She had nothing to lose.

She only hoped that it would lead her to what really happened that night.

CHAPTER FIFTEEN

Daisy had thought that the Vandiveer estate was extravagant and over-the-top, what with its sheer size, gilded statues, and many fountains. But it was a shack compared to the Lafayette estate. Perched on the coastline, the compound featured an imposing, brick wall with actual turrets. The main feature of the house was the giant white belltower. The clock on it struck seven as she approached the gatehouse.

Thankfully, since there had been no murders at the Lafayette estate, the security there was much more relaxed. When she asked to speak with Mr. Hardy, she was buzzed in immediately, and a security guard took her to the main house.

A moment later, the man appeared, dressed in a polo shirt and khaki shorts, looking every bit like an attorney on vacation. He was balding, though tan and not necessarily as mole-like as she'd expected from Coco's description. In fact, his smile was charming, as was his formal British accent. "Good afternoon, Ms . . .?"

"Fortune. Daisy Fortune."

"Ah." He motioned for her to come into a windowed parlor area. Where the Vandiveer's rooms were light and airy, this was anything but. The walls were dark, paneled mahogany, and there was an abundance of red velvet everywhere, especially on the furniture and heavy drapes. It did nothing to let the beauty of the outside in. But what immediately drew her attention were the various life-size, golden lions situated around the room. Zachary must've noticed that she couldn't tear her eyes away, because he said, "Yes, the Lafayettes have rather interesting tastes. Mr. Lafayette collects things from all over the world."

"Oh, they're . . ." *hideous* was on the tip of her tongue, but she remembered her manners, just in time. ". . . Lovely."

He chuckled some more. "Hideous. That's okay. You can say it."

She laughed.

His face turned serious. "The guard out front said that you were a private eye. Are you working for Gireau?"

"No, actually, Natasha Blake hired me."

He raised an eyebrow. "Interesting. I suppose she'd trust a fellow American more. And how are you getting on?"

"Well, still working through the facts of the case, interviewing witnesses. You were there on the night of Jacob Vandiveer's death?"

He nodded. "I'm glad you said death, and not murder, because it was an accident. That's all. The coroner's report confirmed ingestion of fentanyl."

"You seem so sure of that."

"Yes, I suppose I am."

"But a witness said that you were seen outside his room, shortly before he was murdered, and you looked . . . nervous?"

He blinked. "Who said that?"

"Were you there?" she pressed, ignoring the question.

He nodded, then pulled at the collar of his polo shirt. "Yes, I was. Vandiveer had asked me to come aboard because I had papers for him to sign for Vandiveer Holdings. He was in the process of acquiring a mining outfit in Pennsylvania, and I'd been trying to get in touch with him to finalize the documents for weeks. But when I got there, I found out that he was having a pre-wedding party with his close friends and was already three sheets to the wind."

"He was drunk?"

"Very much so. He wasn't coherent in the least. I tried to talk business with him, and he would have nothing of it. Then he and his brother got into a terrible fight over something, and he stormed into his room. When I tried to get him to open the door, he shouted at me to leave him alone. He sounded . . . wounded, I suppose."

"Wounded?"

"Yes. Jacob was the life of the party, but I suppose few people knew him the way I did. He was cracking under the pressure of being perfect for everyone. And whatever Lesley said to him made him go berserk." He sighed. "Accident, suicide. In the end, does it really matter? He was a hurt man. And now he's passed the hurt onto his family. And me. I live every day, replaying that moment, wishing I'd broken the door down, so I could stop him."

"So, you're not surprised to hear that he did drugs?"

"Most people who are constantly on like he had to be use something. I don't judge." He leaned in and said, "You're quite good.

I've been friends with Gireau for quite a while, so I know how he operates. And I think you could give him a run for his money."

Daisy blushed. Was that a compliment? "You think? But Gireau knows everyone, and—"

"Yes, but he's overconfident. He ignores things that don't interest him. He might have a smashing track record here in Rhodes, but he can be a bit daft at times. You seem like a smart young lady, Daisy Fortune." He smiled.

She smiled back. Squirrely? Maybe to someone young and beautiful, like Coco, he was. Balding, with a bit of a short stature, he wasn't a Greek God. But his face was as handsome as any movie star's. Daisy found him genuine, and probably the most down-to-Earth person she'd met since arriving on the island. All the rest of them seemed so pretentious and so out-of-touch with the real world. At least Zachary Hardy seemed to have a grasp on it.

"I appreciate that. Can I ask you what happened after the murder?"

He let out a long sigh. "It was a bit of a mess, that was for sure. The police swarmed the yacht, and we were ushered off into the house where the police interviewed us. Then Gireau came and did the same. Mr. Vandiveer, naturally, was beside himself. He didn't want any guests around the estate. So I decided to come here and stay with the Lafayettes, while I finished my business."

"But you couldn't finish your business? The contracts didn't get signed?"

He nodded. "Ah, yes. No, unfortunately . . . Jacob couldn't. But Franklin Vandiveer still has a stake in Vandiveer Holdings, so he simply managed things."

"So, the deal went through."

He nodded. "Yes, indeed."

That opened up a whole new can of worms. Perhaps the killer was someone who wanted to hinder the deal. Her mind spun with the possibilities. She reached into her bag and pulled out the list. "I just have a few people I haven't yet interviewed. Do you know any of these from that evening? Miranda Castleton?"

His eyes narrowed in thought. "I remember her. Stunning girl. I believe Jacob said she was in from London on her yacht. Quite the adventurer from what I remember. Climbed Mt. Everest, believe it or not. I didn't speak to her. She stayed off to herself, away from the rest of the party. Everyone else at the party seemed to know each other."

"Okay," she said, marking some notes down on the paper. "I'm having a little trouble narrowing down who else was on the ship that night. Natasha wrote me this list, but I think it's in code, because some of the names, I don't recognize."

"May I?" She gladly accepted his offer of help, and he took the paper from her, scanning it. "Oh, well, you're in luck!"

"I am?"

He pointed to the name *Faye.* "That's Jacob's old fencing partner and one of his best mates, Tristan Lafayette. Good chap."

Daisy stared at him. Lafayette. "You mean . . .?"

"Yes, he lives here. I believe he told me he was getting some practice in, but where in this devilishly big house, I don't know." He looked around, then leaned in and said, "I've been handling the Lafayette's affairs for six years, since my father retired, and I still get lost in this place. It's like a labyrinth, except every corner you turn, you're not in danger of finding the minotaur. A heinous gold lion, maybe, but not a minotaur."

She laughed.

He stood up. "Well, come with me. If I was going to have a fencing piste, I suppose I'd have it out on the courtyard . . ." he said, walking in one direction before hesitating and turning in another.

As she followed close behind, she could see what he meant about the Lafayette home. There were more golden lions everywhere: small ones as bookends on shelves and large ones made into planters with ferns growing out their backs. Alone, they wouldn't have been too gaudy, but it was the dark, extravagant velvet everywhere that seemed to make the home like an expensive cave of some long-lost pirate's buried treasure. As they passed an enormous room with a long table and velvet, tufted chairs, which looked something like a medieval banquet hall, Daisy shivered. "This place looks very cold, doesn't it?"

Zachary nodded. "Yes, Mr. Lafayette is a man with strong tastes. He prefers the English castle look. Wouldn't think of letting anyone come in to change it." He rolled his eyes, a small smile on his face.

"And how is his son?"

"Oh, Faye's a character. The jokester of their friend group. They met at school in London when they were boys and were inseparable at once. From what I'm told, they boys were so close that Mr. Vandiveer had his estate constructed not far from this place, so they could summer together."

“Is that right?” she asked, surprised that he seemed to know so much about the families. “You’re a wealth of knowledge on them.”

“I have to be. I’ve managed their affairs for a very long time.” He opened a door out into a vast courtyard. If it wasn’t for the bright, hot sun streaming in from above, she’d have thought that she was in London. She found herself within stone walls covered in climbing vines. It was part grass, part coarse sand, and, of course, there were many statues of fierce lions scattered about.

Across the courtyard, two men squared off with their epees, oblivious to their entrance. Every so often, a grunt of exertion or a “touché” echoed across the yard. Eventually, though, the tallest of the two men removed his face shield and gloves. “Good match,” he said, shaking the other man’s hand.

“Nice match, Faye!” Zachary called.

“As always.” The tall man strode over to them, grinning. He looked over at Daisy, and leaned in, extending his hand. As he did, a lock of dark, curly hair tumbled over his sweat-soaked forehead, shading his eyes. “Tristan Lafayette. But they all call me Faye.”

“This is Daisy Fortune,” Zachary said. “Natasha hired her as a private detective to investigate the business that happened with Jacob.”

His face froze in place for a moment. The news clearly surprised him. “Ah, that so? Good ol’ Natasha. Always taking care of Jake, she was.”

“They had a good relationship?”

He nodded. “Sure. They were a match made in heaven. I introduced them, you know. Was going to be best man at their wedding.”

“Great. Do you mind if I ask you some questions?”

“Not at all. But do you mind if I get a drink, first? I’m parched.” He motioned her to an iron table in the corner of the courtyard, where someone had set a pitcher of water and ornate crystal goblets. He poured them each a glass, then sat down, throwing his equipment to the ground, and wiping his forehead. It was only then that he seemed to notice that Zachary was still there. “Scram, Zach. Let us have our privacy, would you? Go do something legal.”

Zachary nodded subserviently. “I’ll be right inside if you need anything.”

“Doubtful we would,” Faye said, leaning back, taking up all the available space around him with his long arms and legs. He motioned with his chin. “Sit. Make yourself at home.”

She sat, pulled out her pad, and started flipping through it. "Thank you. I just wanted to ask you—"

She stopped when she realized that he was now leaning forward into her personal space. His voice was low. "What did ol' Hardy say to you? That it was an accident? Rubbish."

Daisy tilted her head. "What do you mean?"

"Just what I said. It's rubbish." He spread out his arms theatrically. "The only reason Hardy thinks it is suicide is because Jacob was three sheets to the wind and prattling on nonsensically. He wasn't doing drugs. He wasn't under enormous pressure. That's all barmy. I know, I was his best mate. If there was anything going on, he'd tell me." He jabbed his thumb in the center of his chest.

"And he never mentioned anything like that?"

"No. Not even cold feet over getting hitched. I kept asking him, trying to get him to crack. But if he was upset his bachelorhood days were over, he never said a word to me. Not a word."

"Did he normally confide in you?"

"Oh, yeah. All the time. He told me even before he popped the question to Natasha. He really loved her. He couldn't wait to get married, have kids, be a father." His smile fell. "It was a real shock. And I guess your next question is going to be, who do I think did it, right?"

She nodded. "Do you have an idea?"

"Not a damn clue. We were all having a good time. Drinking. Dining. Talking. It was such fun."

"Did you witness the fight then, between Jacob and his brother Lesley?"

He nodded. "Yeah, but the two of them were always going at it."

"Really? Some people seemed to think that it was pretty brutal, and that Jacob was really affected by it."

"Jacob? Pshaw!" He sat up. "They don't know Jacob. And they don't know Les. I've known them since our childhood in London. Nothing ever bothered Jake. Not a thing. And he and Les were always back-and-forth, getting into nasty roes, throwing things at one another, trying to maim each other . . . and then the next day, they'd be best of mates again."

"Okay . . . so was there anyone there that was behaving oddly?"

He slumped back into his chair, thinking, and tented his hands under his chin. "Well, let's see. The servants: that little dark-skinned chippie, and that fat cook."

Daisy's face fell. "You mean, Adila and Ramon?"

"Right. I don't know the names of the help. They weren't acting odd, but Jake didn't treat them the best. And the blonde one? The one from Sweden or wherever?"

"Milla."

"That's the one. She was always snooping around. So, maybe they decided to do something. Poison his drink? They had the opportunity and the motive."

"Hmm," she said, making a note of that. Though it might have seemed feasible to Faye, there was something about it that didn't ring true to Daisy. Employers enraged their workers all the time, and they lashed out . . . by quitting. *Not* by murdering them. Especially since they'd have nothing to gain. "What do you know about the other people who were there?"

He gulped his glass of water, leaving it next to his lips, and said, "Like?"

She went over her list. "Well, there's—"

"Let's see. I have a great memory. I can tell you exactly who I spoke with and when. I came aboard around six and went to my cabin, put my things in the drawers, and went out above deck for cocktails and games. Coco was there, and Mo, and Rose—those are all Natasha's friends, except Coco, she's Jacob's little cousin. I talked to them a little bit, then saw Hardy and Miranda. We played a few games, had dinner on deck by the pool, and then it was getting chillier so most of us went in. Les was there, I spoke with him a bit, and then we started egging Jacob on. Les was going on about some nonsense about giving up the family fortune, but they started bickering, so I told them I was going off to bed. I did, and slept soundly until the next morning, when I learned that my best mate was dead."

"You were on the ship, in your stateroom when it happened, then?"

"Yes. But dead to the world, from about midnight to ten. Drunk." He shrugged. "So, I'm no help if you're looking to establish exactly when it happened. Besides, my stateroom was on the other side of the yacht."

This line of questioning wasn't getting her anywhere, so she decided to change her tack. "So, what is your impression of the other guests, then?"

He frowned. "Well, let's see. Coco, I've known since she was born. She's young, but she has a sharp tongue. She doesn't let anyone get away with anything. Mo and Rose, I've known them as long as I've known Natasha, which is to say, not all that well, but they seem decent. The marrying type. Les is like my little brother as much as he was Jacob's. Hardy can be a little simpering, because he's not one of us, but my father trusts him, and that's good enough for me." He shrugged. "And that's all she wrote."

Daisy scanned down the list. "Umm, you forgot one."

He blinked. "No. I don't think—"

"Miranda."

"Oh! Yes, Miranda." He snapped his fingers. "Stunning girl."

"Coco said that she was studious and quiet."

"You spoke with Coco?"

Daisy nodded.

"Well, yes, she was quiet. But that was because she didn't know anyone else there. She was no mousy wallflower if that was what she was getting at. Truthfully . . ." He sucked in a breath and blew it out. "I don't know much about her."

"Funny, that was what Natasha said about her too."

He laughed. "Well, maybe you could call her the specter at the feast. To tell you the truth, I don't know why she was invited. She wasn't part of the wedding party. Just an old acquaintance of Jacob's. She'd just dropped in on her own yacht while sailing the Aegean, if I remember correctly. Marvelous sailor, really. She scaled Mt. Everest, he told me. Youngest woman to do so. Jacob really couldn't stop gushing about it."

For someone who professed to know little about her, he certainly did know a lot. And if Miranda had been quiet, the information probably hadn't come from Miranda herself. It had come from Jacob. That struck Daisy instantly. It was a pre-wedding party, with all his family friends, and he was gushing about another woman? Maybe he'd just wanted to help her fit in, but it was odd. "And what did Natasha say about that?"

“Oh, you know ol’ Natasha. Charming as always. It was her idea that Miranda stay aboard the yacht with them. She always puts everyone at home. It’s her specialty, playing hostess.”

Well, it made sense. Natasha was the epitome of cool and collected. But it couldn’t have felt good. Just as she’d done a good job hiding her grief over the loss of her fiancé, maybe she’d harbored jealousy over this Miranda woman?

Or maybe Miranda was jealous over Natasha’s claiming of Jacob. Maybe she’d had designs on the fiancé. That would explain what Coco had said, about them giving each other dirty looks all night. “Was there ever anything between them . . . you know, romantically?”

He recoiled. “No, of course not. I would’ve known. Jacob might have been a playboy before Natasha, but once he met her, that was all over.”

Daisy nodded, but she wasn’t so sure. Miranda might have indeed been a specter at the feast, there to cause trouble. Was it just her, or did Faye know it? There was something disingenuous about his response, the way he looked away and sipped his drink. “Okay,” she said. “Thank you.”

“Just ring me up if I can do anything else for you,” he said with a gracious smile. “Jacob was my best mate, and, of course, I want to know the truth.”

He walked her to the door. When she stepped inside, Hardy was there, waiting for her. Had he been trying to listen in on their conversation? Whatever it was, at that moment, she noticed the sheen of sweat on his forehead, and the uneasy way he cleared his throat as he said, “I’ll see you to the door.”

Now, she understood what Coco had meant. At that moment, he *did* look a bit squirrely.

He guided her through the maze of rooms to the front of the house, and when she stepped out the front door, she expected him to say his goodbyes.

Instead, he looked behind him to make sure that no one had followed him, then closed the door behind him and leaned in. “Did he tell you about the Luvestra investment?”

She stopped. “No . . . what is that?”

He let out an uneasy breath and dabbed his bald spot with a handkerchief. “It was a lithium battery company Vandiveer Holdings had partnered with to begin in China. Natasha had arranged the hookup with some prominent businessmen overseas, and he was pretty keen on it. Thought Luvestra was going to be his ticket. He socked millions into it and got Faye into investing millions as well. But the mines turned up empty, and they lost everything. Faye never forgave him for that, especially since Mr. Lafayette is close to disinheriting him for it."

Her jaw dropped. "He never mentioned a word of it."

"Well, that stands to reason," he said as he walked her toward the street. "Because though I still stand by my theory that it was an accident . . . if it turns out that it *was* murder, I think I'd put Faye high on the list. He certainly has the motive."

CHAPTER SIXTEEN

As Daisy walked back to the Vandiveer estate, a stiff wind had picked up, whistling in her ears. It was that sound that made her think about the specter at the feast.

Out of all of the attendees at the party, Miranda Castleton seemed like the odd one out, the person who didn't belong. Why had she been there? Had Faye been wrong, and she was someone with a dark history with Jacob, threatening to reveal that past to Natasha?

As she walked, deep in thought, she stared at the list, wondering who would know. If Faye, Jacob's best friend, and Hardy, the man who handled his business affairs, didn't seem to know . . . who would?

This time, the guard opened the front gate for her without question. It was dark, now, but the compound was lit up, especially the main house. Every window was alive with light. She might have thought that it was a party, if she didn't know that Franklin Vandiveer had banished most guests from the compound.

Even though she'd been personally invited by Myrtle, she didn't feel like she should be crashing their evening plans. So, she decided to go back to the guest house.

The guest house, by contrast, was dark. As she walked the path to it, she wondered if she'd need a key. But the door was unlocked. As dark as it was inside, she heard noises coming from within as she stepped through the door.

Freezing in the small courtyard open to the sky, she looked into the front rooms of the house. The windows were all open, and gauzy curtains were blowing in the breeze.

Had she opened them? Or had they always been like that?

She couldn't remember. But it didn't matter. The maid, Milla, had fixed up this house the night before. She'd probably been in here, since, straightening.

But the whistling of the wind had taken on an eerie quality. She'd long since stopped believing in ghosts, but she couldn't fight the feeling that she wasn't alone in the house.

Taking a deep breath to calm herself, Daisy felt around the walls, hoping to encounter a light switch. No luck. Eventually, after jamming her shins into a low coffee table, she found a table lamp and pulled the chain near the bulb, casting the room in an orange light.

She sighed and looked around. She was alone.

Even so, she walked around the house, turning on every light she could, just to be sure. All the windows were open, her room had been straightened, her towels had been replaced, and her bed had been made.

That fact made it easy for her to notice a pink envelope atop her pillow. It said, *detective* on it.

She went to it and pulled out a sheet of paper, folded in half, opening it to read the words, scrawled in a shaky script:

there was no wedding!

See the Contentment

Daisy stared at the words, trying to make sense of it. No wedding? Contentment? It felt like a secret code. What did it mean?

As she was wondering, she realized that there was something else inside the envelope. Another sheet of paper. She pulled it out and realized that it was a receipt from a jewelry store. It was a refund for the return of one diamond solitaire engagement ring with a value of over $60,000. And it was dated only a week prior to Jacob's murder.

There was no name on it, nothing at all to suggest that it belonged to either Natasha Blake or Jacob Vandiveer. After all, Natasha had been wearing an engagement ring in her office. She'd never forget that huge diamond and the way it had constantly caught the light with every gesture of Natasha's hands. But it did raise questions. Why would anyone return an engagement ring?

There was only one person left who could provide the answers.

She picked up her phone and dialed Natasha, but the call went straight to voicemail. She left a message asking her to call her back, and sunk down into the covers of the bed, thinking. As she lay there, staring at the note, someone knocked at the front door.

She lifted her head up. "Who is it?"

"Ma'am, it's housekeeping." It sounded like Milla.

"Oh, you can come in."

She heard the front door click, footsteps sweeping along the stone floor, and a moment later, Milla appeared in the entryway to the bedroom. "Just wanted to see if you wanted dinner, or if I could do anything else for you."

Daisy shook her head and lifted the note up. “Did you fix up the room?”

She nodded.

“Did you see this note? Do you know who left it for me?”

Milla said, wide-eyed, “No. What does it say?”

Daisy showed it to her. “And there was a receipt for the return of an engagement ring. I don’t understand. The receipt may not even belong to Jacob. Did anything lead you to think that Natasha and Jacob weren’t getting married?”

Her eyes widened. “All the plans were in place.” She read the note and said. “But this—the Contentment?”

Daisy looked at her. “You know what that means?”

“Yes.” She pointed out the window, toward the marina. “That is the name of Miranda Castleton’s yacht.”

CHAPTER SEVENTEEN

To say that Daisy was up early would be incorrect.

She hadn't really slept at all. All night long, she'd thought about the contents of that note, and about the engagement ring, and wondered what the yacht in the harbor, *Contentment,* would hold for her. Unfortunately, Natasha hadn't called her back, so all of the questions she'd had surrounding the wedding were left to fester in her head.

And who had sent that letter? The answer seemed pretty obvious. If any of the fabulously wealthy residents of the home had something to tell Daisy about the crime, they'd have said it to her face. The only people who had something to risk by revealing the secrets of the Vandiveer family? The help.

So, when she heard someone walking around on her balcony, she jumped out of bed, threw on her robe, and rushed outside.

Adila was there, setting out her breakfast. She jumped slightly when Daisy tossed back the curtain.

"Sorry," Daisy said, coming outside. "I just had a few questions for you. I—"

"Oh, ma'am, you have sunburn!"

She touched her cheeks. Sure enough, they stung. "I didn't notice. Do you happen to have some—"

"The Vandiveers do not, but I have a tube of cream for my hands," she said, reaching into her pocket and handing it to her. "It may help."

"Thank you," Daisy said, looking at the unlabeled tube. It was green jelly, like aloe. It would probably help. "Thanks. I'll use it in a bit. But I had a question. I received a note, and—"

"Note?" she said, looking away to fold a napkin.

In that moment, Daisy knew that Adila had left the note for her. "Yes . . ." she said, wondering how she could get the young maid to admit that she'd been responsible. "It's interesting. But it's not really all that helpful. After all, there's nothing at all on the receipt to indicate it belonged to Jacob Vandiveer."

"Oh, but it was found in his trash," she blurted, before she gasped and covered her mouth.

"Was it?" Daisy said, smiling encouragingly at having made some progress. "Tell me. Why did you write this note?"

The poor creature looked mortified, like she might burst. Her pale face went beet red, tears came to her eyes, and she shook her head. "Please . . ."

"It's all right. I'm not going to tell the Vandiveers on you. Please. Just tell me what you know. Is the ring Natasha's wearing now a fake?"

Adila looked around, to make sure no one was nearby, and whispered, "I don't know. But I know he returned one. There are many secrets in this house that my employer does not want you to know."

Daisy lowered her voice, too. "Like what?"

"Like Tristan Lafayette. No one believes all that nonsense about Mr. Vandiveer building this house just to be close to his old friends, the Lafayettes. He did it because he was having an affair with Mrs. Lafayette, and Tristan—or Faye, that's what they call him—is the result."

Daisy's lips made an O. "You mean that Faye and the Vandiveer sons are half-brothers."

"Did you not notice how they all look alike? The eyebrows." She brushed a finger along both of her dark eyebrows.

She hadn't thought about it, but now, come to think of it, they were very alike in a lot of ways. "Wow. You sure know a lot about the family for someone who has been here only a short time."

"All of their servants know about it, but we are not supposed to talk of it."

"What else do you know?"

"I could stay here all day, but then I would never get any work done." She pointed to the tray.

"All right." Daisy sat down at the table and laced her fingers in front of her. "Just give me a little taste."

"All right." Again, she looked around, making sure they were alone. "Coco? That's not her name. And she's *not* Mr. Vandiveer's niece. In fact, she is not related to the family at all."

Daisy blinked, recalling her conversation with the girl. She'd been sassy and sharp and had never once let on that she was lying. She seemed to fit in so perfectly with the Vandiveers. "Who is she?"

She looked hesitant, but then said, "I suppose you could call her Franklin Vandiveer's pet."

Daisy stared at the young woman, trying to make sense of that. There was only one way to interpret that, and it was twisted. If she was Mr. Vandiveer's live-in mistress, then Myrtle must've surely known of it. Maybe she also knew about Tristan, because that was just who Franklin Vandiveer was—a man with an unquenchable desire for other women. "But Coco was on the yacht, with the wedding party?"

"To keep up appearances. And because she's Franklin's pet, she gets back to Mr. Vandiveer if the boys do anything wrong. She's his little spy."

"His spy? He really didn't trust his boys, did he?"

Adila shook her head. "Funny yes? He is not all that trustworthy himself."

"But why? What reason did he have for not trusting them?"

"I hear Jacob made some bad business decisions. And Lesley, with those silly rockstar dreams? They argue all the time. No, there was no love between the father and those boys." She pointed to the receipt. "Mr. Vandiveer would not have been happy about that."

"About returning the engagement ring?"

She nodded.

"You're saying the marriage of Natasha Blake and Jacob Vandiveer was like an arranged thing? They didn't like each other?"

"I do not think Natasha was very happy." She mimed tilting a bottle to her mouth. "She drank. A lot. When there were others around, they put on an act. But we saw them when they were alone, and maybe they did not realize we could overhear."

By now, Daisy was hanging on the maid's every word. "What did you overhear?"

"That she wanted to call the wedding off."

"*She* did?" Daisy asked in shock. This certainly wasn't the woman who'd come to her office in East Plainfield, asking for help. "But why?"

She looked around and nodded reluctantly. "See the *Contentment.*"

It struck her, just what that meant. "Jacob Vandiveer was having an affair with Miranda Castleton?"

Adila pressed her lips together, and at first, Daisy didn't think she'd speak. But then she said, "Miranda was not happy when she found out he was due to be married. Not at all. There was drama that night before he died. Fights, whispering in corridors and behind closed doors, people taking sides and giving each other dirty looks. It had the air of secrets. And—"

She paused, biting her lip, as if she wasn't sure she should say more. But by now, Daisy knew that she would. Some people simply couldn't keep secrets to themselves, and Adila was one of them. "Yes?"

"I went up to the rooms, late in the evening, to pick up their laundry. This was after one. I never can sleep when the yacht is at sea. I collected the towels from in front of Natasha's room, and she heard me and told me to come in to take some other towels from her bathroom. But as I was picking up the towels from in front of Jacob's room, I heard it. Clear as day." She swallowed. "A woman. Giggling."

Daisy raised an eyebrow. "You think it was Miranda Castleton?"

She nodded. "I don't see who else it could be. But if you ask me, I'd say Jacob Vandiveer was keeping secrets, and where there are secrets, danger always comes of it."

CHAPTER EIGHTEEN

As Daisy made her way down the pier, the dozen or so yachts docked there were so large that they all but blocked out the strong Aegean sun. When she emerged from the shadow of one of the hulking beasts, the sun was so bright, it was like a knockout punch. She blinked, trying to get her eyes to adjust, and saw several men—likely local fishermen— standing on the edge of the parallel pier, pointing and gaping.

At first, the thought that it was an emergency. Pirates. A vessel experiencing trouble. A swimmer, drowning in the sea, which was rougher than usual. But as she scanned the white-capped waves, she saw nothing.

Following their line of vision more closely, she noticed they were staring at one of the smaller yachts anchored there.

More specifically, at the stunning blonde in the tiny, neon-green bikini, who was sunning herself on the bow.

Of course, she thought as a couple of them began to whistle and call to her in Greek. She ignored it all.

Daisy walked closer, checking the names of the yachts, until arriving at the conclusion she'd been expecting the moment she saw the blonde. Her yacht was the *Contentment.* She was Miranda Castleton, the woman who was supposedly having an affair with Jacob Vandiveer.

"Miranda?" she called from below, standing on her tip-toes to see the woman.

The woman didn't even budge. Maybe she was sleeping.

Daisy tried again, louder this time. "Miranda Castleton?"

The woman dipped her sunglasses and groaned. "No, I don't want any, for god's sake. Leave me alone."

She had an air of superiority, like most of the rich and famous, despite her obvious youth. She couldn't have been older than twenty-five.

"I'm Daisy Fortune," she said. "A private investigator. I'd like to ask you some questions about Jacob Vandiveer."

She sat up and removed her sunglasses. The men were still catcalling her, but she didn't seem to notice that. She went to the railing of the yacht and looked down. "Fine. You can come up."

She motioned to a rope ladder that looked rather flimsy. There didn't appear another way aboard. As Daisy grabbed it and tried to put a foot on the rung, it swayed. "Is this . . .?"

But when she looked up, the girl was gone.

Eventually, she managed to hoist her body up and over the rail, only tripping once she'd gotten her leg over. She staggered forward but managed to catch herself before doing a faceplant. She found Miranda sitting by a small bar, sipping a martini and smoking a cigarette.

She tapped the ashes in the ashtray. "What is it you wanted to ask?"

Daisy stepped close to her, looking for a place to sit. There was none, so she rummaged in her pockets, looking for her notebook. As she did, she said, "This is a nice yacht. You don't have servants? Are you the only one aboard?"

She nodded. "I grew up around yachts. I've been sailing alone since I was sixteen. But get on with it, please." She tapped her cigarette on the side of the ashtray, shedding the ashes. "You wanted to know something about Jacob? Have the police learned anything more?"

"Very little. What I wanted to know was why you were here?"

Miranda frowned. "I was in the neighborhood. I just stopped in to see an old friend. Jacob and I met in London when I was going to school there. I thought I'd stop by and see him. That was all."

"So, you had no idea that he was engaged?"

"None. He never mentioned it in our emails and calls. Not that he was trying to hide it, mind you. I was always very busy, and so I never had time for a long chat."

"And how did you feel when you found out?"

"Happy for him," she said with a shrug. "Why wouldn't I be? We weren't romantically involved if that's what you're getting at."

"You weren't?"

She laughed. "No. Of course not. Why else would his fiancé invite me aboard the ship for their little weekend party? It was a gracious thing for her to do, so I accepted. I'd spent a week on the ship, sailing through awful weather, so I was happy to have the diversion. And to spend more time with Jacob."

"So, you're saying it was all very pleasant until you received word of Jacob's death?"

She collapsed on a long chaise behind her, pulled her bare feet up under her, and shrugged. She didn't offer Daisy a seat, so Daisy remained standing. "Pleasant enough. I don't really like get-togethers, drinking and partying and lazing about. I prefer action. But it was fine."

"You didn't see any drama. Any fights?"

"No . . ." She thought for a moment, then smiled. "I can't think of anything. Why do you ask?"

"Well, it's interesting, because I heard from more than one person that there was a fight between Jacob and his little brother."

"Oh, was there? I didn't notice." She looked into her drink, pressing her lips together. "Must've missed that."

"And some people said that things were—how shall I say? On edge? That things were tense."

She hitched a shoulder. "I didn't notice. Then again, it was nice to have the good champagne after weeks of traveling with the junk I'd brought. I might have had a little too much."

Hadn't one of the maids said that she and Natasha had been giving each other looks? And her mannerism and responses . . . they didn't ring true. It reeked of something she'd experienced a lot for the past few days—of someone hiding secrets. Coupled with the news she'd heard from Adila this morning, it was enough to make Daisy suspicious. "You thought Natasha was pleasant?"

"Pleasant enough." She drained her martini glass, then hopped up and went to pour herself another, still not thinking to ask Daisy if she wanted one. Not that she did, but it was a little annoying that she was dismissed so easily. Miranda had simply turned her back on her to head to the bar, without so much as an "excuse me."

But these people didn't ask to be excused. They had been brought up believing that they had to apologize to no one.

So, as she made her drink, Daisy took the time to look about. With modern chrome fixtures and shining wood-paneled appointments, it was clearly an expensive little vessel, but much smaller than Jacob Vandiveer's super-yacht. Obviously, it had to be, since she was the only crew member. It was homier, too, with more personal effects. There were black-and-white, artsy photographs of Miranda Castleton, skiing downhill somewhere in what looked like the Alps, in snow gear at an outpost somewhere, 8,000 miles above sea level, standing on a precarious rock outcropping, miles above a desert landscape, parachuting, surfing, bungee jumping, piloting a plane, holding a fishing pole and a giant swordfish . . . was there anything this woman hadn't done?

"You're a real daredevil, aren't you?" she murmured.

She turned to find Miranda staring at the photos behind her, a proud smile on her face. "I like a challenge. Yeah."

"I heard Jacob really admired you," she said.

"Hmm," she said, with a smile, as if this wasn't news to her at all. "I guess you could say I wasn't what he was used to."

"Meaning, women like Natasha?"

She chuckled. "Natasha, and so many others in our circle, are all the same. Shopping, spa, botox, repeat. I don't care for any of those things. So, I think Jacob admired that."

"Oh? Do you think he was having problems with Natasha?" Daisy asked.

"No. Why would I? I told you, I hadn't seen him for ages prior, and when we spoke, it was superficially. I knew nothing about what their relationship was like."

"Then it would probably surprise you," Daisy said, turning to watch her reaction, "That some witness reported hearing the sound of another woman in his bedroom the night he was killed."

Her eyes went wide. She looked away, the fresh drink in her hand in danger of tipping. "Natasha, of course."

"Not Natasha. The maids are sure of that."

"Oh, well . . ." Her drink finally did tip, and she abruptly straightened it when the liquid hit the top of her bare foot. "That's crazy. It must've been one of the other girls. Those two girls that went to college with Natasha. They didn't seem quite right if you know what—"

"They left the yacht beforehand. With Lesley."

She sucked in a breath. "Oh. Then Coc—"

"His first cousin?" she asked. Though she wasn't sure that was true anymore, she doubted Miranda would know.

Miranda's once-tanned face turned pink. She stood up, went to the railing, and tossed her drink overboard. "This tastes all wrong." She went over to the bar and started to make another drink. "Can you and I speak in confidence?"

Daisy nodded.

"All right," she said, pouring far too much vodka into the martini shaker. "Here's what I know. I got a call from Jacob while I was in

Spain. He told me he needed me to come right away. That he was going out of his mind. Before, there was always the hint that he'd have to marry Natasha. But it was always in the future, never set in stone. When he called me, he told me his father had bought this giant engagement ring and was insisting he make the marriage to Natasha official by the end of the month. Well, he couldn't take it. He told me he wanted to see me one last time."

"So you two *were* romantically involved?"

She rolled her eyes. "If you can call it that. For me, it was just a fling. But sometimes, he talked about forever. He'd say things about how if he could've given that ring to anyone, it would've been me. That's what he told me that night."

"The ring was returned, though. Right?"

Miranda sighed, then tested her drink, and nodded. "He said they fought all the time. One day she'd wear the ring, and the next day, she wouldn't. So, he took it and returned it. Out of spite for her, for his father. He told me he wasn't going to go through with it. His father was furious. There was a huge fight, and it ended with the wedding being moved up. That was when he called me."

"And even though you were there, everything was *pleasant* on board?" Daisy asked, using the word Miranda had.

She sighed. "Okay, maybe they weren't pleasant."

"Did Natasha know about you and Jacob?"

"No. She didn't. But up until that moment, there hadn't really *been* anything between us. It was just a little fun, whenever I was in town. That's all. But that night, everything just boiled over. He told me he had decided he wanted to give it all up. Run away with me. He'd had it all planned out. I told him that he was crazy and that he needed to stop and think. But he wouldn't listen. And he got drunker and more irrational as the night progressed. He and Lesley had a fight—I think he wanted Lesley to take his place at the head of Vandiveer Holdings, and Lesley told him no way. He kept getting more and more touchy-feely with me, right with Natasha there—so eventually poor Natasha had had enough of it and locked herself in her stateroom. I was worried about him, so I locked us up in his bedroom to stop him from doing something stupid."

"Stupid?"

"Yeah. I didn't think he'd kill himself. But he'd ordered the boat back to shore. So, I was worried I—"

"Wait. He ordered the boat back?"

She nodded.

"I thought Lesley did that?"

"No. He did. I was worried he was thinking so irrationally, he might tell Natasha it was over and tell his father to go to hell. And if he lost that business, and if his father disinherited him? That would only make things worse for him."

Daisy gave her a narrow-eyed look. "So, you're saying you were trying to save him from himself? So, you didn't sleep together?"

She shook her head. "I mean, we *did.* Several times before, whenever I was in port. Like I said, it was a fling. We didn't that night, though. He was such a mess." For the first time, she looked sad. "I just wanted to help him. But I couldn't."

"So, what happened? When did you leave him?"

"Two. Maybe two-thirty. He was asleep, at the time. Or . . ." She swallowed. "Maybe he wasn't. Maybe he was dying. I remember thinking it looked like such a deep sleep, like he was so peaceful, I didn't want to disturb him. Until then, he'd been drinking whisky, in bed, going on and on about how he wished things could be different. And then, eventually, he just passed out. I thought he was drunk."

She put her hand to her face, and for a second, Daisy thought she might begin to cry. But she simply swept a lock of hair from her face. Still, when she spoke, that air of superiority was gone, and her voice was weaker. She sounded almost . . . like any regular person. A person with regrets.

"I don't know where he'd gotten the drink from. When I heard that he'd died of fentanyl poisoning, I kept trying to remember where it'd come from, but . . . I can't."

Daisy paced the deck, imagining the scene. Yes, if a man was distraught and drunk, the logical thing would be to pack them up to bed so they could "sleep it off." It wouldn't occur to most people that a lethal dose of a drug had been consumed, if they left before the victim stopped breathing. "He brought the drink up from downstairs, then?"

She nodded. "That, I'm sure of. He didn't have a bar or any alcohol in his room. I know that his friend Faye was bartending, before. So, it could've been him, but I'm not sure."

"You don't think it's suicide, then."

"No. Not with the way he was talking. He was sad about his future, but he still thought there could be a way to get out of it, to run away with me." She let out a sad laugh. "Even though I'm never getting married, part of me wished that I'd agreed to it. If I had, maybe he'd still be alive."

When Daisy had stepped aboard, she'd all but decided Miranda was guilty, and that it had been a crime of passion over losing her man to another woman. But now, she wasn't so sure. Her story made sense. So, either Miranda was a very good liar, or what she was saying was true.

"Thank you," Daisy said, going to the railing where the ladder was attached. After her struggle to get up, she was already dreading going down. "You'll still be in port if I have any questions?"

She held up her martini glass and nodded. "For the next few days, anyway. I don't have any plans."

Daisy swung a leg over the railing and carefully made her way down to the pier. When she reached the bottom, she stumbled a little, but even the catcallers were gone, and she was all alone.

As she walked back along the beach, dreading the climb up those long stairs to the house, her phone buzzed with a text. She fished it out of her pocket and read:

Natasha: *Darling, I'm shopping downtown. Marvel at Rhodes Palace.*

CHAPTER NINETEEN

"I'm sorry, ma'am, but I can't let you through."

Daisy stood in front of the store with the mirrored walls, looking desperately at her reflection. The man standing in front of the doors was almost twice her size and wearing a tight sweater that showed off biceps the size of dump trucks. His arms were crossed in a threatening manner.

"Yes, but I'm trying to explain that I was asked to come here," she said, standing on her toes to look past him into the door, which had the only non-mirrored window inside. "If you just go and—"

"This is a private shopping experience, ma'am. We only allow one client at a time." He ran his eyes down her, stopping at her sensible shoes. "I do think the shopping center on Ocean might be a better fit for you, no?"

She sighed, wondering why, if this place was as secure as the Alamo, Natasha hadn't told them to expect guests. Well, she didn't have to wonder too long. It had obviously slipped her mind in favor of more important things. "For the last time, Natasha Blake asked me to meet her here. If you can just go ask her . . ."

He frowned. Then he tapped his earpiece and spoke aloud. "Linda, we've got a woman here who says she's a guest of Natasha Blake. A Miss . . ." He gazed at her expectantly.

She'd given the name before, but he hadn't been listening, so the next time she said it, it came out with a huff. "Daisy Fortune."

"Daisy Fortune." He paused for a moment, listening. Then, finally, he stepped aside and pulled open the door for her. "You may go in."

"Thank you," she said, giving him a haughty, *I-told-you-so* look.

When she stepped in, she felt like she'd entered a giant castle. This was no ordinary department store. In fact, there were no racks or cash registers or signs indicating anything was sold there at all. The walls were all mirrors, and the floor was a shiny pale wood. There were a couple of rather ugly purses and scarves on display behind heavy glass security cases and some misshapen, headless mannequins posed in strange ways on pedestals throughout the vast room.

From the back of the room, a couple of very well-dressed saleswomen with pointed features stared at her as if she'd lost her way. No offers to help.

As Daisy was trying to decide where to go, a voice called, "Darling!"

Natasha was emerging from a room in the back, which must've been a dressing room, because she was wearing an all-white suit outfit with almost comically wide pant legs and a matching floppy hat. Of course, with her figure and posture, Natasha pulled it off, making it look elegantly chic. She spun in front of a set of mirrors, then stood on a pedestal to admire herself as Daisy drew near.

"What do you think?" she asked, striking a pose as the other women gathered around her, oohing and aahing.

"Nice," Daisy said with a smile, thinking the question was directed at her. She hated to think how much that ensemble probably cost.

But then a voice from the corner mumbled, "It makes you look like a goddess," and she realized that Maureen was there, sipping champagne and looking otherwise bored.

Natasha motioned to the saleslady in the same way she often motioned to Daisy. "I'll take this one, too," she said.

"Yes, Ms. Blake, absolutely," the woman said, bowing slightly as Natasha tossed her the hat like a frisbee.

"Any news yet?"

This time, Daisy looked into the mirror and saw Natasha's eyes were fixed on her. "Well—"

"Goodness, what is wrong with your face?"

Daisy frowned. That was nice. Now, everyone was looking at her. She peered in the mirror across the room and realized her cheeks, where she'd applied the aloe cream Adila had given her, were bright red, almost as if she'd been slapped. "Oh, I—"

She waved her off. "You were saying? About the case?"

"Yes, there have been some developments . . . but—"

She whirled. "There have been? You know who killed my beloved?"

Daisy blinked. After everything she'd heard, "Beloved" was taking it a bit too far. But she supposed that after the fact, when there was no chance of them marrying anymore, it was a nice thing to say. "No, not yet. But I found some new information."

Natasha put her hands on her hips. "Well? Spit it out."

She cleared her throat and looked around uncomfortably. She wasn't sure Natasha ever actually *got* embarrassed about anything, but what she had to share would ordinarily embarrass most people. "I did call you. I had a question to ask, and—well, do you think we could speak in private?"

Natasha looked around and seemed to be surprised that she had a small entourage of people watching her. "Fine. Come in the dressing room with me."

She jumped off the podium and disappeared between two accordion doors.

Daisy wasn't sure she wanted to be caught in a stuffy little room with Natasha as she undressed. Besides, in every department store dressing room she'd ever been in, it wasn't exactly private. Despite the closed doors, everyone in every room seemed to know exactly what everybody else was trying on and how they felt about it.

But it turned out that she didn't have to worry in this store. The dressing room was almost as big as the entire front shopping area of the store. There were chairs set around the perimeter of the room, and discarded clothing all over the floor. Natasha shimmied out of the white jumpsuit and went to the mirror, dabbing at the rash on her neck. "Now, what was it you wanted to ask me?"

"I wanted to ask you about your ring."

"My ring?" She laughed and looked down at it as she stood there, unabashedly, in a matching red bra and thong. "What about it?"

"Well," she said, trying to figure out how to pose the question as delicately as possible. "Did Jacob ever return it?"

Her eyes met Daisy's. "What? Of course not. Why would he . . .?"

"Well, I've heard that there might have been some trouble between the two of you. That maybe he'd been having second thoughts?"

She shook her head. "Oh, no. Never. In fact, the night before he died, he told me he couldn't wait for me to be Mrs. Vandiveer. He was that excited about it."

"I heard that you had a fight. That there was tension."

"Between Jacob and his brother, yes. We spoke about that. But that was because he thought Les was being silly, wanting to forsake the family by pursuing his childish whims. That's all."

"It wasn't because he'd asked Les to assume the family business, and Les refused?"

She threw the white jumpsuit on the ground like a piece of trash. "Who told you that? Why would Jacob do that? He was born for the business, and—"

"There was a rumor that the pressure to perform for his father and live the life his father had set out for him was too much. That he was planning to run away." She pulled out the receipt and unfolded it in front of her. "Or at least, he wanted to. With Miranda Castleton."

Natasha stared at the receipt, not moving.

Then she closed her eyes and swallowed. "All right. Yes. Things were not perfect between me and Jacob. He wasn't my first choice of a man, that was for sure. But we made sense. He knew it, and I knew it. But when he looked at forever, he got scared. He was being irrational and having doubts—and yes, he sold the ring. I saw that he was in danger of destroying everything, and I didn't want that to happen. So, I had this fake made up, so that his father wouldn't question anything. I knew that if he took his time, he'd eventually realize that the life his father wanted for him was the one he wanted too. So, I did what I always did as the good fiancé. I did everything possible to save him from himself. I covered up the cracks and tried to buy him time with his father. And when Miranda showed up, I suggested she come along so that he got her out of his system."

"But he didn't get her out of his system."

She sighed. "He *was*. He would have. I'm confident that if he was alive today, he'd have made the right choice. But someone took him from us before he could."

Daisy flipped through her notes, not sure she wanted to bring the next point up. "I've just confirmed that Miranda Castleton was the last person to see him alive. She was in his room at two in the morning on the night of his death."

Natasha's eyes flashed to hers, full of fire. "What? That bitch!" She stalked across the floor, then spun, clenching and unclenching her fists. "Don't you see? She knew he was changing his tune, that he didn't want to be with her anymore, and so she killed him! A crime of passion! She murdered him because if she couldn't have him, no one could."

Daisy nodded. It certainly was one plausible explanation. "Yes, that's possible, but—"

"It's definite! I can't believe—" She stared past Daisy, as if forming her own plans. "Call the police. She thought she could go in there and sweet-talk him away from me, huh? How did you find out? Was it one of the maids?"

"Miranda Castleton told me, herself. She said that she, too, was trying to save him from himself."

Natasha scoffed. "Oh, did she? By murdering him?"

"She said he was depressed about being forced to do his duty for his father and wanted to run away, and she was trying to prevent that from happening."

"I'm sure she was. What a little saint she was," she snarled bitterly, throwing up her hands. "And I was trying to be nice, inviting her aboard. I never should have. I should've sent her back off to sea the moment she arrived."

She slumped down into her chair and covered her face with her hands. For a moment, she said nothing.

When she looked up, her face was streaked with tears. "It's my fault he's dead. I let her in."

Daisy sat next to her on the chaise and went to pat her shoulder as some sort of gesture of comfort, but Natasha flinched uncomfortably, so she stopped an inch short of touching her. "Now, don't get too carried away. We still don't know how he was poisoned. He was drinking whiskey, which probably had the fatal dose, if so, he must've brought it from downstairs, which meant that anyone could have poisoned the drink."

"But *she* did, obviously. She had every reason to. Clearly."

Natasha was right, but Daisy wasn't so sure. She didn't get the impression that the young woman had been lying. Maybe she had wanted Jacob dead because she felt betrayed and couldn't see him with another woman. But then again, she seemed so independent. When Miranda had said that she didn't want to be tied down to another man, Daisy believed her.

Besides, there were plenty more people who seemed to favor Jacob a lot less.

She stood up. "From what I hear, a lot of people had a reason not to like your fiancé. So, I can't rule them out yet."

"To me, it seems pretty cut and dry," she huffed, slipping into her slacks. She pulled on the rest of her clothing and stood to step into her designer heels. "But you do what you have to do. I just hope that we can have an end to this soon."

"I'm doing my best."

She strode to the floor-length mirror and touched her face, fixing her make-up. Then she rummaged through her purse, pulled out a vial, and spritzed *Vivante* all over her face and neck. "Well, remember, I'm not paying you to go on vacation. I want answers. You've been here two days, and I haven't gotten a single one."

"I'll have more soon."

"Good." She waved her off. "Now go. You're dismissed."

Daisy stared at her for a moment, feeling humiliated, before retreating through the accordion doors. Once again, the women in the store ignored her as she made her way to the exit.

As she took a cab back to Makarios, Daisy's head started to ache. She'd been feeling pressure to solve the case before, but with Natasha's words, she felt even more strained. She had all the stories of the people who'd been on the *Fantasea* the night of the murder, and yet, all of them seemed to contradict one another. Everyone who professed to know Jacob clearly hadn't known him well at all, because nothing about him was clear. Either he abused drugs, or he didn't. Either he was a demanding jerk, or he wasn't. Either he wanted the life his father had laid out for him, or he didn't. Either he'd been having a mid-life crisis, or he hadn't. The question bounced around in her head, hitting her skull harder than ever:

Who was Jacob Vandiveer, really?

She looked over her list. There was only one other servant that she hadn't yet interviewed, and that was Ramon, the head chef. According to Myrtle, he had been with the family forever. Maybe he could shed some light on who the victim really was.

But when the cab pulled up to the front of the estate, there was a police officer stationed outside.

As she got out of the car and went to the front gate, he stepped in front of her. "Are you Daisy Fortune, the private detective?"

She nodded.

"Place your hands behind your back. You are under arrest."

CHAPTER TWENTY

The only jail cell at the downtown police station in Rhodes had crumbling walls, a single barred window that was so high, and no furniture except a thin, lumpy mattress on the dirt floor.

As Daisy sat in the corner of the cell, counting the spiders skittering past her feet, she wondered what she'd done to deserve this. Apparently, in Rhodes, they were allowed to bring you in without telling you what your offense was. When she'd asked, she'd been yelled at in Greek. The only thing the police officer had managed to say to her, in horribly broken English, was a threat: "You know no one here. We can just make you disappear."

Their presence hadn't been very reassuring. After that, she'd just complied and let them bring her into the downtown jail. She'd been sitting here an hour, assessing her life and what had brought her to this point.

One thing seemed clear. Now, any hopes of finding the killer had been dashed. Natasha would be furious with her, Gireau would prevail, and she'd be sent back to America and the failing Fortune Investigations with her tail between her legs.

As she sat there, staring at the floor, she thought of her father. It wasn't long ago, when she'd checked him into Independence Court, that she'd reassured him that she'd hold down the fort with Fortune Investigations. He'd been so reluctant to leave his business, his baby, but he'd had to because of that mysterious illness. She'd told him that she would keep things going. But she hadn't just wanted to do that. She'd wanted his business to thrive, to become what it had been in the olden days when he was young and respected among even the most elite people in the country.

But under her ownership, business at Fortune Investigations had only gotten worse and worse. She was failing Edward Fortune, and that thought was what stabbed at her heart the most.

She pulled her knees up to her chest and had just lowered her forehead to them when the prison bars clanged open. Zachary Hardy appeared. He was dressed in a more attorney-like ensemble than earlier, a suit with a sedate red tie, polished briefcase in hand. "There you are. Are you okay?"

"What are you doing here?" she whispered in shock and relief. "How did you—"

"Myrtle told me," he said shaking his head as he lowered a hand to help her up.

"You're my attorney?" she asked, wincing. He didn't seem like the type to work pro bono, and whatever he cost, she probably couldn't afford.

"No, no, you're free. Charges have been dropped. Ol' Franklin might have a lot of power, but even he can't bypass the rule of law in this case."

She gaped. "Franklin Vandiveer did this?"

"Yep. He might be able to get the police to do his bidding, but a lot of what he asks of them is not technically legal. And since you weren't trespassing, they can't hold you. Myrtle told me to come down and get you."

"Thanks," she said as she followed him out. A guard handed her a plastic bag with all of her personal items inside, and they strode out into the afternoon. "I don't understand why he had me arrested."

"Because he thought you were poking where you shouldn't have been. And then Gireau probably agreed with him, and that was all it took." He motioned her to his car, a tiny, silver-blue convertible sportscar. "Come on, I'll drive you back."

She hesitated. "I don't think I have anywhere to go. I've been officially shunned from Makarios."

"Actually, you do," he said as he unlocked the doors for her. When she stared at him in confusion, hoping that Natasha had decided to put her up in that posh Hotel Rhodes, he smiled with clenched teeth. "Apparently, Gireau has summoned us to Makarios."

Her gut dropped. "Why would he do that?"

"That's Gireau. He likes to have an audience."

She swallowed as she sunk into the buttery leather passenger seat of his sportscar. "For . . . does he think he knows who killed Jacob?"

Hardy's lips twisted. "Yes," he said softly. "It's likely he does. He asked the media from the mainland to be there as well, and he probably wouldn't have done that if it was anything else. While it's good news, I'm sure it's disappointing for you."

Though everything inside her was coming apart, though she wanted nothing more than to ask him to drive her to the nearest airport so she could go home as soon as possible, Daisy tried to keep a stiff upper lip. "Well. At least the Vandiveers will have their answer."

"Yes, I suppose."

As they drove, she looked out the window at the bustling shops of downtown as they gave way to the more exclusive homes and hotels on the shoreline. Maybe she should've just been happy to come to this place, to explore Rhodes. She never thought she'd ever investigate a crime in a place so fancy and exotic. And not only that, a murder. Plus, if Natasha didn't demand her fee back, Daisy still had the deposit she'd received.

But none of that made her feel better. She'd wanted to solve this case and prove that she was worth her salt as a PI.

Even before they reached Makarios, Zachary whistled. Daisy looked up to see red tail-lights stretching into the distance, and people lining up at the gates. "What the . . . ?" he said, pulling to the side of the road and cutting the engine. "We'll have to walk it."

Daisy followed him to the front gate, where a small crowd of people had gathered. She stayed close behind as he wove his way through, trying to reach the guard. The moment the guard saw him, his expression softened. "Mr. Hardy," the guard said, motioning him in.

"What's all this?" Zachary asked the guard over the roar of the crowd.

"You know Gireau," the guard said. "He told everyone he was going to make a major announcement in the case . . . except the Vandiveers. When Mr. Vandiveer found out, he was furious. The last thing he wanted was for this to be a circus. I'm under orders to keep everyone out."

"What about us?" Hardy motioned to her and himself.

"You're clear." The two of them moved forward and stepped through the small opening in the gate.

Then they ran ahead to the house. Despite the guards working to keep people out, it seemed quite a bit more crowded than in the previous days. There were luxury cars parked around the fountain, and a few people were standing outside, smoking. As she drew closer, Daisy recognized them as Coco and Faye.

"Hey, if it isn't the old gumshoe," Faye said, with a wink. "Guess Gireau bested you this time, huh?"

She forced a smile. "Well—"

"Wait a second. Let's listen to what the man has to say. He could be totally wrong," Coco said, swiping one of her loose blonde pin-curls behind her ear. "I mean, he created this shitshow, when he should've known better. Vandy's not happy."

Faye laughed. "Gireau's always right. Just ask him."

Daisy went inside to find all of the usual players assembled in the living room. It looked like a scene out of mystery movie, where the famous detective gathers all the suspects and reveals the killer. Luckily, Vandiveer hadn't allowed any media in. He and Gireau were arguing in the corner, Gireau gesturing grandly and talking about the gratitude he was due for bringing the case to a successful conclusion. Everyone else was sitting silently around the room, looking confused. The two housekeepers were there as well, passing out tea.

"Please, can we get on with this?" Myrtle said, teacup on her knees, looking uncomfortable.

"Yes," Les said, his upper lip curled in disgust. "All this fanfare is ridiculous. Just let us know what happened."

Mr. Vandiveer broke from the Gireau with a wave of his hand. "All I know is that I wasn't paying you for a performance. I was paying for answers."

"And you'll get them, soon," Gireau said with a smug smile on his face. "But we cannot begin until Jacob's fiancé arrives."

Lesley let out a groan as Gireau stepped up to Daisy, his smug smile deepening. "Well, hello. You came to admit defeat?"

She stared at him, speechless.

"Don't worry. I think this will be good for you. You will learn how a real detective works, eh?" he said, looking over her head and clapping his hands and catching sight of something behind her. He shouted, sharply, "We begin now!"

At that, Natasha swept in on a wave of heavy *Vivante*, making the entrance to end all entrances. Everyone spun to look at her in her black scarf and tight black dress. Scratching a long fingernail under the scarf, she swept her eye over every person in the room with disinterest. Then she looked at Daisy and let out a sigh. "Well," she spoke sarcastically, rolling her eyes. "I see my money with you has been well-spent."

Lesley patted the sofa next to him. "Sit here, Natasha," he said, and as she did so, Daisy noticed Miranda staring daggers at her from across the room. A moment later, Natasha lowered herself into the chair and began to return them.

Coco came in and stood next to Mr. Vandiveer, who'd lowered himself into a high-backed dining chair. She put a hand on his shoulder. "This is ridiculous. It's hurting the family. Can't you see that?"

Myrtle snorted. "*You're* honestly talking about hurting the family?"

Gireau stood amongst them and clapped his hands. "Enough!" he shouted. "Now, I will tell you what I know."

Zachary had moved inside with Faye, and was now sitting up close with the other members of the Vandiveer clan, but Daisy didn't feel like she belonged there. She hovered in the doorway, leaning against the jamb, waiting as the man paused for dramatic effect.

It continued for so long that she rolled her eyes.

Then he said, "I did not arrive easily at my conclusion, I will tell you. But once I had interviewed everyone, the solution became crystal clear. Maybe not to you, but to my trained eye, it seemed quite obvious what had transpired on the night of Jacob Vandiveer's death."

Daisy stared at him, her mind threatening to wander. Could he possibly drag this out any longer? Everyone was sitting there, leaning forward, hanging on his every word. And Girard strode about the floor in his patent leather shoes and suit, looking completely in his element.

She scraped her top teeth against her bottom lip, fighting off the envy welling up inside her. *He's an overstuffed, overimportant windbag,* she told herself, but that didn't stop her from wishing she was there, instead.

Gireau held up his hands. "Now, I know there was a question as to whether Jacob took his own life, or whether it was an accident, or whether he'd been murdered. So let me settle that, right now."

He paused.

Or sometime in the next week, Daisy thought, now completely unable to stop herself from sighing in desperation.

The pause was overly pregnant, seemingly going on forever as he spun in a circle, scanning the faces of the people around him. He seemed to delight in having their undivided attention.

"I deduced quite quickly that it couldn't have been suicide as the police scoured the *Fantasea* after Jacob's death, and there was no trace of fentanyl anywhere aboard. Also, from my conversations with his family, I don't believe for one second that Jacob had ever been suicidal in his thirty-one years."

From her vantage point, Daisy could see every person's reaction. Myrtle nodded in agreement. Miranda's lips twisted. Franklin Vandiveer harrumphed. "I said that," he muttered. "He was a Vandiveer."

Coco patted his shoulder. "Okay, so then, was it an accident?"

"No," he said, pausing once again to take in all their reactions. If this had been a TV movie, it would've cut to commercial break right then. His eyes lit up, full of joy at this exciting reveal, even though by then, everyone knew what was coming.

It was just the words, spoken aloud, that he knew would chill people to the bone, and so he waited. And waited.

And then, he said, drawing out every word and spinning in a circle so he could make sure everyone heard him correctly:

"It. Was. Murder."

CHAPTER TWENTY ONE

The words hung in in the air, echoing around them.

Myrtle gasped and clutched her heart, but beyond that, everyone was completely silent.

Daisy looked up at the ceiling. None of this was really news to her or anyone else. Now, it would just be another excruciatingly long wait for him to reveal the name of the actual killer.

Finally, Faye broke the quiet. "All right. Get on with it. Who was the killer?"

But Faye had to have known that the detective wouldn't simply spit it out that easily. No, he would drag it out again, wait until they were salivating. Daisy was sure of that.

As she expected, he began to pace, his hands laced together at the small of his back. "Let me take you back to when I first arrived at the crime scene, the morning Jacob's body was found in his stateroom."

Myrtle brought the teacup to her lips, her hand trembling. "I wish you wouldn't. I don't want to relive that day anymore."

"Ah, but my dear," Gireau said with a smile. "It's necessary. You'll see why in a moment. Now, as I was saying, when I arrived, I noticed at once the whiskey glass was on the ground, and it was quickly decided that whatever was in that glass had killed him. Late that evening, after the fight with his brother, someone made him a drink which he took up to his stateroom with him. By that time, most everyone on the yacht was either ashore or in their own stateroom. There was only one person who was left in the room, and that person poisoned the drink and helped an inebriated Jacob Vandiveer back to his room."

Everyone looked around at one another. Finally, Franklin Vandiveer said, "All right? Who?"

Daisy groaned and stretched her back against the door jamb, preparing for another painfully long wait. But the seasoned detective must have been too excited about his own find, because he jabbed a finger in Miranda Castleton's direction and shouted her name so loudly that the reporters at the front of the compound, nearly half a mile away, probably heard.

Miranda stiffened. “What? Are you insane?”

“It is true,” he said, beginning his pacing once more. “I am sure without a shadow of a doubt. *She* was the one observed by servants in his stateroom shortly before his death. *She* was the one who made his drink. *She* was the one in whose stateroom the police found the fentanyl, and *she* was the one who was having an affair with him!”

Natasha snarled, “You . . . you were sleeping with my fiancé? When I took you in, took care of you . . . and this is how you repay me?”

Everyone stared at Miranda, waiting for her to explain herself. She glared right back at them. “That’s garbage. I told you, I didn’t have, and have never had, a supply of fentanyl. If you found it in my things, it must’ve been planted! And as far as my relationship went with Jacob, we had had a fling in the past, but as far as I was concerned, it was over. I was friends with him. That’s all.”

“So, you deny that you were in love with him? That you came all this way looking to rekindle your relationship with him, only to find him engaged? That in your jealousy, you decided to take action and make sure that if you couldn’t have him, nobody else could?” His words shook the walls around them.

“Absolutely. I deny all of that,” she said, staring him down. “We were friends. With benefits at times, but I never wanted anything more. It’s the truth.”

“Why did you drop everything and come here from Spain when he asked you to?” he demanded.

She looked around. “I received an urgent message from him. He told me that he wanted to talk to me. I thought he might be in trouble, so I came to help him. As a friend. Then I found out that he was getting married soon and unhappy with taking over the business, and wanted to put the brakes on everything.”

“That’s bullshit. Jacob lived for that business,” Franklin Vandiveer grumbled. “You killed my son.”

“I swear, I did not!” she shouted, but all at once, the room erupted with raised voices, all fighting against one another.

Daisy pushed away from the wall and moved closer to the fray. “I don’t think that’s right,” she said in her normal voice, but it was easily drowned out by the cacophony of yelling.

She went up to Gireau, who seemed to be delighting in the chaos he'd created, and spoke, "Are you sure? I don't think Miranda did it."

He glared at her. "I'm always sure. Of course she did it! She was in his room at the time of his death. Even a mediocre PI would've known that."

She shook her head and shouted as loud as she could over the crowd, "Lesley, what did you and Jacob argue about before you left the yacht?"

He stared at her, stricken. "What? I told you, I—" He looked over at his father. "Nothing."

"I have several witnesses who said that Jacob *was* distraught last night. He was having cold feet about something," she announced. "And if no one saw who made the drink, he very well could've made it himself."

They all stared at her.

"What I'm saying is that we have no proof that Miranda did this," Daisy said. "We just have a bag of fentanyl that anyone could've planted in her stateroom."

Gireau frowned. "And she was in the room with him at the time of the murder. That's more than enough."

"Assuming it *was* murder," she said, crossing her arms and meeting his smug smile with a challenge.

Franklin Vandiveer stood up. "Enough of this. Enough of this all. This whole thing has turned the Vandiveer family into a laughingstock, and I won't have it. This ends, now." He glared at Gireau. "I don't care. There was a substance. It somehow got into his drink. It was an accident. That's all. You understand?"

No one spoke. The man commanded the room like a drill sergeant. When his eyes swept over Daisy, she felt her heart pound.

"I don't want the media here anymore. And I sure as hell don't want any more private eyes snooping around here. Have I made myself clear?"

Again, no one spoke. No one moved. It seemed as though no one breathed.

"You two—I want you out," he pointed to Daisy and Gireau, and then to the door.

Gireau said, "Now, Mr. Vandiveer, don't be—"

"Out!" He said, so sharply and loudly that half the room jumped. "You'll get your check by mail."

Daisy turned and went for the door. When she was outside, she breathed a sigh of relief. She wasn't wanted at Makarios. She'd have to go pack.

As she took a step toward the guest house, Gireau appeared at the top of the steps, his hands wrapped around the lapels of his blazer. "Some people," he said with a shrug. "Cannot handle the truth."

"How do you know for sure that that is the truth?" she asked him. "It seems too obvious. Why would anyone hold onto the fentanyl if they'd just murdered someone, knowing it would incriminate them? She could've simply thrown it—"

He waved a hand at her. "Oh, stop. I have made my determination. If they won't accept it, it's their problem. My next step is to bring my findings before the local police. But my work here is done. Good day."

She watched Gireau stride toward the gates. Her work here was done, too, whether she wanted it to be or not. She was no longer welcome here.

Her father's voice echoed in her head as she turned toward the guest house. What would he have done? Well, that was easy. He would've marched in there and told them that the case had not been solved. He would never let the conclusion be "an accident" unless every stone had been turned. And it still felt like there were more avenues to pursue.

But she was not her father. She didn't have the respect that came with successfully solving hundreds of cases.

And now, maybe, she never would. Her father would say, *You have to start somewhere.* She'd hoped that this case would be the one that was the start, the one that leveled her up to real detective work. But she'd failed. And now, she had to leave.

As she walked to the guest house, someone called to her. It was Zachary Hardy. He stopped short in front of her, out of breath. "Are you okay? I feel bad for the way Vandiveer treated you in there. All you wanted to do is help."

"It's okay. I guess I'm not needed."

"No, you *are*. Gireau presented his findings and wouldn't let a soul attempt to poke holes in it. But you found the holes. And that means the mystery is still unsolved. Contrary to what Mr. Vandiveer thinks, none of us will ever rest well if we don't know what really happened that night."

Daisy shrugged. "But what can I do? They want me out, and I don't have any new leads to follow."

He looked hesitant for a moment, then peered around to make sure no one was nearby. "I might have something new."

"What?"

"Well, it's something Faye told me a while ago. Everyone knew Jacob was a playboy, most of his life. The going story is that once he was engaged to Natasha, he quit all that. But it wasn't entirely true, was it? He was still carrying on a relationship with Miranda," he said with a shrug. "I didn't want to say anything because I don't think it's my place to speak ill of the dead, but I've been thinking about something I heard Faye said to him once, not that long ago . . ."

"What did he say to you?"

"Well, it was a couple months ago. He had a deal going through, and he was stressed, and Jacob was talking about how Natasha was away in the States. I remember specifically because Jacob shushed Faye after he said it, but he said, 'I'm sure you'll have something to de-stress you,' and looked, kind of suggestively, at the maid that was serving us dinner. I didn't think anything of it at the time because Jacob was a new man who'd turned over a new leaf. . . but now that I know that's not true, I have to wonder . . . was he also having an affair with one of the staff?"

Daisy nodded. It was possible. And entirely possible that one of them could have slipped in to easily poison the drink, since they were used to being invisible. "Which one?"

"The light-haired one. I'm sorry, I don't know her name."

"Milla," Daisy murmured. "Thank you. I'll check it out."

He smiled. "All right. Good luck. Be careful."

The door to the main house opened, and some of the family began to filter out. If she was going to investigate Milla before they forced her out, she had to make it quick.

CHAPTER TWENTY TWO

Rather than take the path that led to the guest house, Daisy took the one that brought her to the patio. A small, shaky staircase led her down to the bottom floor of the main house, where the staff quarters and kitchen were.

When she appeared at the door, all of the cooking staff looked up in surprise. Whatever they were making smelled delicious—like olive oil, rosemary, and roasted meat—but the staff didn't look like they were in any mood for compliments. A large woman in a hairnet shook a rolling pin at her and shouted in Greek, flour flying everywhere.

"I'm sorry!" she said. "I'm looking for Milla?"

The old woman continued to scream at her, making her step backwards. She was about to retreat when a man came forward. "Wait, wait. I know this woman," he said, raking his eyes over her in a way that felt like she was being mentally undressed. "You're that PI, right? What do you want with Milla?"

Daisy caught her breath and relaxed a little. "I just have to ask her a few questions."

He motioned toward a narrow corridor. "She's on her break right now. She should be in the last room on the right."

"Thank you," she said, following his directions. The door at the end of the narrow corridor was closed. She knocked, but there was no answer.

She decided that she would already be in trouble if Vandiveer found her here after his orders to vacate the property. So taking a deep breath, she pushed the door open an inch. When she peered inside, she saw a small, neatly-made wooden bed with a white, embroidered duvet, and a small nightstand with a reading lamp on it.

She pushed the door open and saw a high, six-drawered dresser. A battered suitcase was lying atop it, open so that its top rested against the wall mirror. The case was full of clothing.

It looks like she was planning on going somewhere. Why?

Daisy scanned the room. Though it was far less opulent than the rest of the home, it was similar to Jacob Vandiveer's in that except for the suitcase, there was nothing personal about it. She went to the case and, since she felt guilty going through the woman's private things, only moved aside a few items before determining it was just clothing and toiletry items and deciding to try elsewhere.

She opened the dresser drawers, finding them empty, and turned to the nightstand. That drawer was empty too. It definitely looked as if Milla was leaving. Did it have anything to do with the crime?

Something was missing. It didn't make any sense. Where was her passport? Her wallet? Her other personal things?

As she spun, feeling hopeless and like her moments were ticking away, she caught the reflection of the top of the suitcase in the mirror. There was a zippered pocket there. She went and opened it, then slid her hand inside, touching paper.

The first thing she pulled out was a folded letter. She opened it and found a scrawled handwritten note that read:

M, I'm sorry things had to work out this way. You know I care about you but we can't continue this because of who I am, and what I need to do. I hope this last check is enough and we can put this behind us, though I promise I'll never forget what we had. Yours, J

She stared at the message. J . . . was that Jacob?

Milla was having an affair with Jacob. Was she blackmailing him too? It seemed the more she learned about Jacob Vandiveer, the more out of control his picture-perfect life was. And it was all his own doing. As if he, like Natasha, went searching for the drama.

As she was standing there, letter in hand, the door opened more. Milla came in, carrying her toothbrush and toothpaste. Her eyes caught on Daisy.

Without warning, she dropped her things, spun, and took off in a run.

Daisy went after her, racing down the corridor and back into the kitchen. The cooks there all looked stunned. Daisy skidded to a stop and looked at both doorways—the one to the outside and the steps to the main part of the house—trying to decide which route Milla had taken. "Where did she go?"

Ramon pointed up the stairs. "What did you do to her?"

Without answering, Daisy raced up the stairs, taking them two at a time. Again, she came to another doorway, and a long, arched hallway. Breathing hard, she looked down the hallway. No sign of Milla. She listened, hearing the rapid tapping of footsteps on the stone floor to her right, and took that route. Sure enough, she found herself in a familiar area, the main part of the house, with the fountain and courtyard.

Then she heard Myrtle screech, "Milla! Milla, dear . . . what are you doing?" and the sound of breaking china.

The next thing she knew, Daisy barreled into the living area. She hadn't expected it, but people were still congregating in that room, drinking tea. Adila was on the ground, picking up a broken teacup, and everyone was staring toward the front door, Myrtle murmuring about how she didn't know "what had gotten into that girl."

As Daisy took a step forward, all eyes swung toward her.

Franklin Vandiveer's voice boomed at once. "You!" he said, his face turning red. "I told you to—"

She managed to side-step him, and artfully dodge her way around all the other Vandiveer friends and family, as well as the antique furniture, and rush for the door. She heard the front door slam shut just as she was reaching the courtyard.

Daisy threw open the front door and raced out into the dying light of day. Looking around, she caught sight of Milla, rushing toward the steps leading to the marina.

Daisy picked up the pace, reaching the staircase when Milla was nearly halfway down. She was clearly an athletic girl, with the way she was taking the steps as if it were no trouble at all.

Where is she going? There is no way out unless she plans to swim or hijack a yacht.

"Stop!" Daisy shouted at the top of the stairs, cupping her hands around her mouth. "Milla, stop! I just want to talk!"

The assurance did nothing. Milla continued to take the stairs at a breakneck pace. At one point, Daisy watched in horror as the young maid seemed to tire, break her rhythm, and slip on a narrow step, stumbling forward. She managed to grab the rail to steady herself and continued on.

The staircase was a danger, even when taking care and going slow. Running? It was a disaster waiting to happen. But she had no choice. Taking a deep breath, she began the descent, keeping her hand close to the railing.

As she ran, she kept an eye on Milla. The maid reached the bottom of the stairs and began to run across the beach, kicking up sand as she went, her long braid flying out behind her like a kite's tail. She was headed straight for the marina.

Daisy reached the bottom steps, finally, and took off after her. There were a few fishermen at the pier. Gulping for air, Daisy asked them, "Did you happen to see a maid? Braid, black dress?"

They shook their heads and shrugged, not meeting her eyes.

They're lying. Of course, they thought they were protecting her. "Please," she begged. "Are you sure?"

She spun, shielding her eyes from the dying sun, looking for the maid. She found her, down the pier, removing ropes that tethered the ship to the dock, then trying to scuttle up the ladder up onto Miranda's yacht. She must've known that with Miranda up at the main house, there would be no one aboard.

Daisy raced to her and grabbed her by the ankle before she could reach the top. She yelped, lost her grip on the ladder, and fell backwards. The only thing there to break her fall was Daisy. When Milla fell back, Daisy caught her, then the two stumbled backwards in an awkward dance that the maid clearly had no desire to be a part of. She flailed, elbowing Daisy in the chest. "Let go!"

Daisy managed to tighten a grip on her shoulders and wrestle her to the ground, despite the maid gnashing her teeth and pinwheeling her arms and legs like a wild animal caught in a trap. Straddling her, Daisy grabbed her wrists and held them down to the wooden dock. "Don't move! I just want to ask you some questions."

Without warning, she spat in Daisy's face.

Daisy recoiled in shock, but did not let go. It was hard to believe this was the woman who'd been so attentive to her needs while she'd been staying at the guest house. "Were you having an affair with Jacob Vandiveer?"

"Let me go!" she continued to shout, her feet scraping on the wood planks as she thrashed. "I did nothing wrong!"

"You were attempting to steal Miranda Castleton's yacht, weren't you?"

She stopped flailing and spat out, "I was trying to get away from you."

"I want to ask you about that note. Were you having an affair with Jacob?"

Milla snorted. "We were not having an affair," she announced defiantly. "We were in love."

When Daisy was sure that the woman wasn't going to fight her, she loosened her grip. "In love? But you were blackmailing him too?"

"At first. I walked in on him once with that woman. Miranda. And he was paying me to keep quiet, so that his fiancé would not find out," she said. "But eventually, we fell in love."

"And then? Why did he send you that note?"

"That father of his was insisting that he marry Natasha. He was too much of a coward to break things off with her. And so, he tried to buy my silence. Send me away."

"And you couldn't let that happen. You loved him and couldn't stand the thought of him with someone else. So you killed him," she said, all the pieces falling into place in her head.

Her eyes narrowed. "No. I did not kill him. I loved him."

"Liar!"

They both looked up to see Natasha marching down the pier, the fire of hell in her eyes. "You kill my fiancé and then you try to steal a yacht? You little witch! What were you trying to do, get some of his money? All this time!"

By now, more of the Vandiveer party was coming down the pier toward them, flanked by several police officers. Since there was no getting away now, Daisy got to her feet. Milla did too. "I did not!"

"I knew you. You were always listening in at doors, listening to our private conversations. I thought it was strange, how whenever I found Jacob, you were close behind. You deny that you were having an affair?"

When Milla didn't answer right away, a smug smile on her face, Natasha pulled back and slapped her across the face.

"We were in love!" Milla said, thrusting her chin out. "And I did not kill him. I have been mourning his death since I heard of it. Which is more than can be said for you."

"Ridiculous. You ruined my life." Natasha motioned to the local police. "Take her away."

The police scurried forward to do as they were told. Milla protested, claiming her innocence again and again, but she did not fight when they cuffed her and led her away.

Natasha ignored her and turned to Daisy, a smile on her face.

"Good work, Daisy." Natasha spun and headed back down the pier, her hips swinging, leaving only the scent of her perfume behind.

Daisy smiled. It was the first compliment she'd ever received from Natasha Blake. The first big case she'd ever solved on her own. And now, she'd have the money and a little bit of a reputation to keep Fortune Investigations going. It was a good thing.

But why did Daisy feel so queasy, suddenly?

CHAPTER TWENTY THREE

As Daisy stood in the bedroom of the guest house, packing her meager belongings into her bag, there was a knock at the door.

"Come in," she called, looking around the room. It was spotless. Milla must've made it up shortly before she was arrested. She may have been a killer, but she was still a good maid too. It was hard to believe that someone could have gone through all that over love and jealousy.

When she looked up, she saw Myrtle standing there. She smiled. "You did a good job. I'm sorry my husband was not so hospitable. But we are grateful to you."

"Thank you," she said. "I'll be out of your hair in a little bit. Natasha's arranging a car to pick me up and take me to the airport."

"Oh, there's no rush," the woman said sweetly. "We really appreciate—oh, goodness!"

She froze, looking at Daisy—really looking at her—for what felt like the first time. Her eyes seemed to be stuck on something slightly below Daisy's eyes. She touched her face as the woman shook her head.

"You have blisters there. What is that?"

Daisy felt it gingerly. "Oh, it was just sunburn. But Adila gave me some gel to use, and I don't know what it was. But I think I might be allergic because it's getting all blistery."

Myrtle made a tutting sound with her tongue. "Sit down, sit down."

Daisy did as she was told, setting her backside on the bed as Myrtle stood and looked at it. "What you need is some good first aid cream. I used to be a nurse, in another life, believe it or not. I can get you some in the main house if you'd like?"

"It's not really necessary," she said as Myrtle made a closer inspection.

"Oh, but it looks so raw!" the woman trilled, shaking her head. "It's those knock-off companies. They make things that are supposed to be just like the real thing, but they're nothing like the real thing."

"Oh?"

"Yes, I remember when I was young and struggling, I wanted a brand of face cleanser that all the movie stars were using. But it was too expensive, so I bought a substitute that was supposed to be the same ingredients, and oh, did my face break out! They use shoddy ingredients so when you think you're saving a few bucks, it's never worth it."

Daisy stood up and looked at her face. Most of the blisters had popped, and now it was just red and raw. She'd seen far too many people, lately, with similar rashes. Maybe it was an epidemic. "I can't believe a simple cream could do some much damage."

"Not just creams. Sprays, perfumes, different food you eat. You really do have to be careful about what you let near your body, these days . . ."

As she stared in the mirror, something came to her. Natasha had had a rash on her neck too. She'd used that fancy perfume, *Vivante.* Maybe she was allergic to it.

Or was it really *Vivante*?

Don't be silly, Daisy. Of course it was real Vivante. Natasha Blake is as rich as they come. Why would she ever need to look for a knock-off?

That question was still marinating in her mind as Myrtle said, "Are you all right, dear?"

Daisy looked at herself. Her cheeks looked even pinker, now, because the rest of her face had gone completely white.

"Myrtle," she said, thoughts and past conversations now stirring in her head like a soup, "What do you know about Natasha Blake?"

She blinked. "Natasha? Oh, well, she came from a very good family. She's a bit . . . how shall I say? . . . icy, but—"

"What do you mean?"

"Well, when Jacob died, she couldn't bother to stay around even for the funeral. She said it was too depressing for her, that it hurt her too much, but—missing your own fiance's funeral? I understand that the two of them weren't a match made in heaven. It was set up because the Blake family has a great fortune and uniting the two families would have been advantageous to—"

"Do you know the Blakes? Have you met them?"

"No," she said, frowning. "I mean, Franklin . . . we were going to meet for the wedding, and—"

"Didn't they meet in college? Wasn't Natasha part of his crowd?"

She shook her head. "That was the official word because it looked good for the papers. The truth is they only started courting a few months ago."

"So, you really don't know if Natasha Blake is Natasha Blake?"

Myrtle laughed. "Of course she is. You don't think that the New York City Blakes made up their daughter? She's famous, well known, and incredibly wealthy and poised. All of society knows her name."

"But not her face," Daisy whispered.

Daisy's breath caught in her throat. If what she thought was true, then she'd just accused the wrong person of murder. She needed to think quickly to set it right.

"Mrs. Vandiveer," she asked, gnawing on her lip as she looked out at the *Fantasea*, floating out on the Aegean. "Do you think I can use the yacht tonight?"

CHAPTER TWENTY FOUR

As the sun set over the island, Daisy stood on the bow, leaning over the railing, thinking.

The more she'd researched, the more certain she'd become that Milla was not the killer. No, she'd learned plenty about the Blake family. They were as private as the Vandiveers, due to various scandals that had besotted the family. Sometimes, that privacy was a good thing. But in this case, it had allowed one particular scammer to take advantage.

At least, that was what Daisy thought.

Now, she just needed to confirm it.

She took a deep breath of chilly evening air as she watched Natasha Blake step into a motorboat and navigate her way toward the yacht. She was wearing that white jumpsuit she purchased earlier and a chiffon scarf over her head. Daisy was surprised she'd even accepted the invitation. She thought she'd be long gone. But now she understood something. She was still hoping to stay in the Vandiveer's good graces. All Daisy had had to do was mention that Myrtle and Franklin Vandiveer wanted to give her the *Fantasea* as a token of their friendship, and she'd jumped at it.

Daisy went down the steps and to the master suite where Jacob had been murdered. It had been neatly made up, but a little shiver passed through her as she thought of him, lying there, breathing his last breath.

As she sat down on the edge of the bed, Natasha walked in, tapping her index finger against her chin as if she was making plans to change all the décor now that she was the sole owner. Her eyes landed on Daisy, and she frowned. "What are you doing here?"

Daisy smiled. "I suppose I should ask you the same question."

She looked around, confused. "Where are the Vandiveers?"

Daisy folded her arms over her chest. "Actually, they're not here. I wanted to talk to you, first."

She snorted. "Well, I don't want to talk. Weren't you supposed to be on a flight home? I'm in the process of wiring you the money, so you can—"

"You don't really have any money, do you?" Daisy asked.

Natasha stared at her for a long time before laughing again. "What do you mean? Of course I do. The plane? The clothes? Everything? You think that's all a mirage?"

"I think you created it all yourself. I think it's all a carefully crafted disguise to make people think you are Natasha Blake when you are nothing but an imposter."

She laughed again. "I am, am I?"

"Because of the perfume."

"Oh?" She tapped the side of her face. "You mean my *Vivante?"*

"But it's not real *Vivante*. It's giving you a rash every time you spray it. Because you just wanted to be the illusion of an heiress. You're not really one."

She scoffed. "I'm not? Then who am I?"

"I don't know. But you're not Natasha Blake." She pulled up her phone and ran through the articles she'd seen on the Blake family. "Sixteen years ago, Natasha Blake was stalked and harassed, nearly killed by a stranger, and after that, her family pulled out of the public completely. They've been off the grid since then. And you decided to use that to your advantage."

"Oh, really?" Natasha said, her lips twisting in amusement. "And why would I do that?"

"Because you knew that you would be able to make a match with Jacob Vandiveer. Somehow, you convinced him that you were Natasha Blake, and in that way, you could secure his millions."

She leaned forward, interested. "Hmm. Fascinating. So I killed him? Before I married him? Now, tell me, how would I get his money, doing that?"

"Because of Luvestra."

Her smug smile disappeared. "I have no idea what you're talking about."

"It was the reason Franklin Vandiveer didn't trust Jacob anymore with his money. The Luvestra deal, to make batteries in China. You got him and Faye to invest in it, and then, when the deal fell through, something tells me you were on the receiving end of the money they lost." From the look on Natasha's face, Daisy knew that she was right. She matched her look with a smug smile of her own. "Tell me, was there even a Luvestra at all?"

She rolled her eyes. "There was, but it was only three of us, and none of us knew a thing about any lithium mine in China. Because I was the one sticking my neck out the most, I got fifty percent from the deal. Barnesy and my driver each get twenty-five."

Daisy smiled, encouraged. She couldn't back down, now. "Jacob found out about it, didn't he?"

She shrugged, and the next time she spoke, there was a marked difference in her accent. The hoity-toity silver screen movie-star voice was gone, and she suddenly sounded like a common girl from Long Island. "That night, yeah. He overheard me talking to one of my associates. Took him long enough. I thought he'd be too embarrassed to admit to anyone he'd fallen for such a scheme orchestrated by his own fiancé, but do you know what he did? He said he was going to tell everyone. And obviously, I couldn't have that."

"So, you killed him."

"Naturally," she said with an indifferent shrug. "If anyone found out about Luvestra, and that I wasn't Natasha Blake but Carly Rutherford, a simple scammer from Brooklyn . . . I'd lose all that cash I'd banked."

Daisy reached slowly into the pocket of her cardigan, feeling for the phone. She really hoped she'd pressed the right button and that it was recording right now. "How did you do it?"

Natasha shrugged off her jacket and started to pace. "Well, after he got rid of that Miranda girl, I went inside. He was still so drunk that he had no idea. I simply opened his mouth and sprinkled a little on his tongue." She motioned to the bed where the body had been found. "He woke up in time to see me, and I made like a good little nursemaid and helped him wash it all down with a glass of water. I imagine the fentanyl worked pretty quickly after that. Though I've never had to use it before, I kept it around in case of emergencies. Then, when all the commotion was going on, I planted the packet in Miranda's bag."

Daisy slid off the bed. She didn't want to be close to this monster of a woman. "So, why didn't you run off when you got the money?"

She snorted. "Why didn't I? Because I wanted to ride the gravy train as long as I could until it went off the cliff. If I'd have married him, I'd have made a mint, but Myrtle Vandiveer indicated that she was willing to 'help me out in the future,' since I've been such a great friend to the family." Natasha, or Carly, batted her eyelashes innocently, and then grinned slyly. "What can I say? I'm greedy. A little bit more money and I can retire nicely to the islands and live the rest of my life in luxury."

"You killed Jacob, though," Daisy said, hardly able to believe she could be so cavalier and heartless.

She waved a hand through the air. "Of course I killed Jacob. Oh, there are always sacrifices to be made. People say kindness is key, but in the end, it really is survival of the fittest. I learned that when I passed my first bad check at sixteen. And I've been doing it ever since."

"But a maid is going to hang for the murder you committed. I can't let that happen."

Carly's eyes narrowed. "Oh, yes you can."

Daisy shook her head. "I'm sorry, but there is no way that I can just let this go."

"I think you can, Daisy," she said, pulling a small pistol from her bag and aiming it right at Daisy's chest. "Whether you want to or not. You *will*."

CHAPTER TWENTY FIVE

Daisy raised her hands over her head in alarm and cursed inwardly. Her father never would've been so stupid as to get into a situation like this. She'd walked right into this trap. Now, here she was, alone, with a killer. And there was nothing to stop Natasha Blake—or Carly Rutherford—from killing her right now.

"You don't need to do that," Daisy said, her voice trembling.

She cocked the gun and tightened her finger on the trigger. "I think I do." Then she giggled. "Oh, Daisy, I didn't think it was going to be this way. When I told Myrtle I was going to hire my own private eye because I desperately needed closure in Jacob's death, she ate it up. She thought I was so caring, so considerate, that I couldn't bear to not know what had happened to my fiancé. I knew that if I did that, no one would ever suspect me of killing him. And I was right."

"Until I came around," Daisy muttered, her gut sinking. Once again, it was her fault. The failure of her business was enough. But her failure this time would cost her own life.

"That's right!" Natasha said, the point of the gun never wavering. "When I went into that shabby office of yours, I knew I'd found the right place. I thought that whoever worked there had to be so galactically inept and useless that this would be fun. I mean, if Gerard Gireau was having trouble, I figured if I brought the most worthless PI in, there would be a ton of entertainment value in it. And there was! You two were really hilarious, walking around, chickens with your heads cut off."

Her smile fell.

"But then you had to go and do this. You had to go and solve the damn thing." She laughed. "A shame for you. Doing all this work, for nothing."

Something occurred to Daisy. "Are you saying the money that was deposited in my account as a down payment was . . ."

"Oh. I hope you didn't already have it spent. That'll probably bounce . . . soonish? Not that it matters for you." She laughed. She looked around, shaking her head. "So, what? Are you telling me that you just made that up, about the *Fantasea*? That Myrtle and Franklin don't want to give me this yacht?"

Daisy shook her head.

She clenched her teeth. "Damn. Ain't that a bummer? I loved this yacht. It would've been perfect for cruising the Caribbean with. Oh, well." She pointed the gun at Daisy's head, then her chest, as if trying to decide where to put the bullet. "Maybe, if I tell them I came up here, saw you trying to make off with the yacht, and shot you to keep you from getting away, they'll give it to me then? It's possible."

"Please . . ." Daisy begged, her blood running cold. She felt sweat dripping down her temple, and her knees went weak. She thought of her father, who she'd never get to say goodbye to. He would never know what happened to her. And from that point on, he'd be desperately alone without anyone to visit him. Her gut swam as she gasped, waiting for the dark barrel of that gun to fire. "Please . . ."

There was a sound, coming from outside, one she couldn't quite place amidst the splashing of the waves against the hull of the ship. It was a scraping sound. A moment later, a spark of hope ignited in her when it came again. *Is there someone out there?*

But it might have just been her imagination, her desperation giving way to fantasy. Carly clearly heard nothing because her smile widened. "Oh, don't beg," she said in her theatrical Natasha voice. "It's most unbecoming for a lady."

"Hello?" a male voice suddenly called out from the corridor.

It was Daisy's moment, and she wasted no time in grabbing it. She lunged for the gun, taking it in both her hands, just as the shot rang out in her ears.

CHAPTER TWENTY SIX

Daisy didn't have time to wait for the pain to register. She and Carly Rutherford stumbled back to the plush carpeting of the *Fantasea's* master suite.

Maybe a woman like Natasha Blake wouldn't have had the street smarts to get into a fistfight, but Carly Rutherford certainly did. The gun skittered off somewhere. Daisy saw it in the periphery of her vision, slipping from Carly's manicured fingers, before disappearing altogether. Before she could swing her focus away, Carly threw a punch to the right side of Daisy's face that made her teeth rattle in her skull. Seeing stars, she pulled back for only half a second before resuming her wrest for control.

Daisy's hand found the woman's face, and she pressed down on it to keep her from getting up as she flailed beneath her. Carly's teeth gnashed, biting hard on Daisy's little finger. Daisy screamed and pulled away, which allowed her assailant to get the upper hand.

The woman Daisy once thought was an elegant debutante was deceptively strong. Even in her designer white pantsuit, she managed to roll Daisy over until she was on bottom. *I'm losing this fight,* Daisy thought as she stared up into the slitted eyes of the woman whose face was red and twisted with rage.

The more she fought, the more tired she became, and now, Carly's full weight was sitting atop her chest. Her lungs were being crushed. She tried to suck in a breath but found herself unable to. She couldn't move her arms, so when she felt Carly wrap her hands around her neck, she knew that it was over.

The pain in her lungs was an explosion. She wanted to fight it, but she couldn't. She thought of those many days she used to spend under her father's desk at Fortune Investigations. She thought of the first case they'd gone on together, as partners. She thought of the many things he'd taught her, none which seemed to be applicable to this situation. But she'd learned so much. He'd been so patient with her, molding her to take over the Fortune Investigations dynasty for him.

And it was going to end like this.

She never thought she'd ever feel homesick for a place like East Plainfield. But now, with her whole life flashing before her eyes, she did.

She closed her eyes and felt her strength, the world, draining away.

"What the—what's all this?" a British voice called from the doorway.

And then, suddenly, the pressure was gone. She gasped so deeply that her lungs couldn't handle it, and she wound up choking and rolling to the side, trying to get her lungs to work again. When she cracked open an eye, she saw Zachary Hardy backing Carly Rutherford up against a wall. He had the pistol, and her hands were raised in surrender.

Thank god, she thought, because she could not speak. Her throat ached. Something pulled her eyes closed.

The next few moments came in flashes, like scattered snapshots. She couldn't be sure how much time passed between each. She heard him calling for the authorities. In the next flash, he hovered over her, eyes full of concern, trying to smooth back her hair and check her pulse. "Do you hear me?" his voice, soothing and welcome, asked her, but she could not answer. Later, the room was flooded with men in dark uniforms, some standing over her, checking her out.

"Ms. Fortune?" one of the men said. "Can you hear me?"

This time, when she opened her mouth, she was surprised to find that her vocal capacities had returned. "Yes."

They helped her to sit up. She blinked, head pounding and vision swimming, and grabbed the back of her head.

"How do you feel?" one of the men asked.

"I'm okay. Just a headache, I think."

Zachary sat on the bed. "You should let them take you in and evaluate you."

She shook her head and struggled to stand. If the experience had taught her anything, it was that she never wanted to leave her father without letting him know where she was going ever again. "No . . . I need to get home," she said. "My father . . ."

"Wait . . ." Zachary laughed, incredulous. "What's going on here? Why were you fighting with Natasha Blake?"

"Oh . . ." The weight of the case hit her all at once. She'd almost forgotten. "Natasha. Her real name is Carly Rutherford, and she's a fraud. Where is she?"

"A fraud?" he asked, incredulous. A couple of the other officers were listening in now too. "She's in police custody. Did she have something to do with—"

"Yes." She reached into her pocket and pulled out her phone. "She murdered Jacob Vandiveer to prevent him from disclosing a deal she was behind that she profited from. I have her full confession here."

Zachary's eyes went wide. "You mean, Luvestra? Surely that's—"

She pressed play on the recording, hoping she'd gotten it all, and thankfully, Carly's voice came through, loud and clear: *Of course I killed Jacob. Oh, there are always sacrifices to be made. People say kindness is key, but in the end, it really is survival of the fittest. I learned that when I passed my first bad check at sixteen. And I've been doing it ever since.*

One of the officers who was listening said, "Can we get a copy of that?"

She nodded.

"You said her name is Carly Rutherford?"

Daisy nodded and typed the name into her search engine. The first result was a mugshot of a woman who'd been nabbed in San Francisco for money laundering. Her black hair had been bleached white-blonde and with terribly dark roots, she had raccoon eyes, and looked like she might have been on something, but it was undoubtedly the person they knew as Natasha. She showed it to Zachary, whose eyes widened.

He scrolled some more. "Blimey. She has a list of prior convictions longer than the Thames. She's a dodgy character, for sure. Whoever would've thought it?"

Daisy nodded. "It seems that she's been pulling the wool over the eyes of the Vandiveers for quite a long time. Not to mention that the real Blake family probably knows nothing about this. It's hard to believe that she got away with it for so long, but as you can see, she'd a professional fraudster."

"Well, she's going to be going away for a long time, now," the officer said, making a quick exit.

Zachary helped her to the deck of the ship and helped row her to dry land. When she stepped onto the pier, police cars had gathered, and Carly Rutherford was in the back of one of them, glaring at Daisy.

She sighed. If anything, Daisy should've been glaring at her. Carly Rutherford had upended her existence, brought her halfway across the world, and nearly ended her life. Now, she had to go back home . . . how? She didn't even have the money in her account to buy a plane ticket home.

"Is everything all right?" Zachary asked her as he helped her down the pier. "Your head all right?"

She nodded. The pain in her head was nothing like the pain in her wallet. How much was a ticket home from Greece? Maybe she had enough space on her credit card. She hoped she did. But she was too embarrassed to confess such a thing to Zachary. "Just . . . thinking about getting back home."

"Ah. Well, I'm sure the Vandiveers will be grateful," he said. "I should stop in and tell them the latest developments, and then I'll be happy to give you a ride to the airport?"

"Thanks," she said. At least she wouldn't have to spring for cab fare. "That would be great."

CHAPTER TWENTY SEVEN

Unfortunately, Zachary was wrong about the Vandiveers.

There was no pomp and circumstance when Daisy got into the car to head to the airport. No waving, grateful fans to see her off. Daisy had been in the guest house, packing, but according to Zachary on the drive to the airport, they'd been less than enthused by the apprehension of Carly Rutherford for Jacob's murder.

"You can't blame them," he'd said, giving her a reassuring smile. "They'd wanted to remain private to avoid people who'd taken advantage of them, but they'd just spent the better part of a year falling victim to one of them. And she took their eldest son from them."

Daisy had understood. These rich and famous types didn't just suffer privately. When there was a scandal, all the world watched it unfold, made assumptions, and passed judgement. It was enough to make her glad she didn't have much money in her bank account.

Well, almost.

Luckily, she'd had enough space on her credit card to pay for the $3,000 last-minute coach airfare from Rhodes to Philadelphia, with two stops along the way in Athens and Frankfurt. She knew she'd probably spend the better part of . . . well, forever, paying it off. But it couldn't be avoided. She also knew that it would be hard to find a way to string together the money to pay Independence Court for her father's next month of care.

But she would make do, just as she always did. Somehow.

She actually found herself smiling as, after twenty hours of travel, the plane finally touched down in the good old US of A. She was alive. She had proven to herself that she could solve crimes, just like her dad, even if she got no accolades out of it. And she would survive.

Even if it meant closing up shop and finding another job. She wouldn't like it, but she would do it. If it allowed her to spend time with her father and give him all the care he deserved, it would be worthwhile.

***

The following day, Daisy pulled up in front of the barred windows of the Fortune Investigations building. Navigating around a few discarded garbage cans, she pulled out her key, rolled back the security gate, and unlocked the door. She stepped in, smelling the familiar, yet comforting scent of old coffee, her father's cigars, and mildew, then crouched to pick up the few envelopes that had been forced through the mail slot.

Bills, bills, and more bills. One, for the electricity, had a bright red stamp on it that said, *FINAL NOTICE.*

She flipped on the lights and was surprised to find that they still worked.

But not for long. Eventually, since she didn't have the money to pay, they'd go out.

Daisy walked farther into the room, past the many empty desks, to her own. She dropped the mail on her blotter and looked at the phone. The red light on the voicemail wasn't blinking.

No messages at all. In four days, the number of people who had called looking for a private eye was zero.

She swallowed, trying to remind herself that this was a good thing. Soon, it wouldn't be her problem. Soon, she'd have a huge weight off her back. She'd cast off that albatross. She'd spent most of the flight, and a long, sleepless night prior, making the decision.

The business couldn't continue. It was time to close up shop.

If she explained that to her dad, as much as she hated to do so, he would understand. She just needed to get out from under her pride. She'd always wanted to be the perfect daughter. But he'd never expected that of her. That was a burden she put on herself. She just had to face him and tell him what had happened.

Yes. He'd be hurt, but he would be okay.

And so would she.

She went into the back of the office to put on a fresh pot of coffee, since she was definitely going to need it today, as she went through the business's affairs, trying to decide what had to be done in order to close Fortune Investigations.

When she returned, bringing the too-hot coffee to her lips and pulling back suddenly as it burned her tongue, she was just about to mutter a curse when she looked up and saw a large form standing in the doorway.

The curse she'd planned to speak turned into a little cry.

As her eyes adjusted and his face came into view, she realized that she knew the man standing there in a dark coat and plaid scarf, looking more like he belonged on Wall Street. He had a healthy island tan, and his salt-and-pepper hair was slicked back from his forehead.

It was Franklin Vandiveer.

"Hi," she began cautiously, sure this was going to be another tongue-lashing. What was he going to do now, accuse her of destroying the guest house or one of his precious Ming dynasty vases? She really couldn't put it past him to travel 5,000 miles just to give her a good piece of his mind.

But his voice was uncharacteristically quiet and meek. "Hello, Ms. Fortune," he said, and she was happy that he didn't recoil in disgust at any of the furnishings as Natasha—Carly—had. He pointed at the same over-taped, battered chair that Natasha had sat in. "Do you mind if I sit?"

"Knock yourself out," she said, setting her coffee next to her overdue bills and sitting in her own chair. "You've come a long way."

He nodded. "Yes. I took my private plane."

"Nice," she said, managing a smile. She remembered Carly's private plane. She wished she'd relaxed and enjoyed that experience a little more, because now, she really doubted she'd ever get a chance to do it again. She laced her fingers in front of her. "How can I help you?"

He cleared his throat. "It appears that you left before our business with you was finished."

"Oh?" She remembered the cold stares they'd given her as she brought her bag to Zachary's car. "I'm sorry. Did I leave something behind?"

"No. We expected you'd come back, though. You have to understand that the Vandiveer reputation is of the utmost important to us. The past couple of days, we were expecting quite the media storm. But that didn't come to pass. And I have to say . . ." He cleared his throat again, as if he was having trouble getting his next words out. "We appreciate your discretion in the matter."

She blinked. Wait. Was that an actual . . . compliment? "Oh. Uh . . ." She blathered for a moment, completely speechless. "No prob."

"Well, Gireau wouldn't have been quite so discreet," he said with a slight smile. "So, I wanted to tell you that."

Still rattled by the man's sudden awkwardness, she found herself being even more awkward in return. She gave him an enthusiastic thumbs-up, then cringed at how stupid she was acting.

"Anyway, Hardy told me that you likely didn't get paid since Natasha—Carly—was the one who commissioned you to investigate," he said, standing and reaching into the pocket of his coat. He produced a check, which he handed over to her. "I hope this will cover everything."

She stared at all the zeroes on the check. Five of them. And a one. $100,000. She had never seen a check so big in all her life. Her jaw dropped. "Are you . . ."

"Also," he said, looking around. Meanwhile, Daisy winced, sure he'd realize what a hack she was and take the check back. But he did no such thing. "You will be getting a call from a dear family friend. It's another case. He should be contacting you shortly. He's in the Caribbean, I believe."

He extended his hand for her to shake.

"Oh! Sure!" she said, lunging forward to grab his hand. She nearly knocked her coffee over onto the bills and the check but managed to catch it just in time. She shook his hand heartily. "I will be here."

As they shook hands, his eyes seemed to catch on something behind her, and he raised an eyebrow. She knew what was coming next. The thing that would make him realize what an imposter she was and completely pop this dream that she was having.

Instead, he said, "Ah, Ed Fortune, huh? I remember that case. This is his outfit, hey? You're his daughter?" His eyes lit up like a kid on Christmas, and the next time he spoke, he sounded like a starry-eyed fan, meeting his childhood hero. "No way."

"Yes, way," she said, smiling. "And thank you, Mr. Vandiveer. You have the assurance of Fortune Investigations that we will always remain discreet in our services."

EPILOGUE

After Daisy paid her mounting bills for her apartment and the business, as well as for the next few months of care for Edward Fortune, she wound up with just enough to buy herself an extravagant meal at the Thai restaurant down the street.

Back to the old grindstone, she thought as she stepped into her apartment. She'd just finished visiting her father at Independence Court, and he was well. The money from the Vandiveers had been a reprieve, but now, she had to strategize how she was going to keep Fortune Investigations afloat for the next few months.

More clients would be a good thing.

She was sat down with a carton of pad thai and the local paper, flipping it open until she found the ad she'd placed. At one point in time, Fortune Investigations had taken out full-page ads in glossy, well-known publications, but all she could afford was a tiny, three-line ad in the LOCAL SERVICES section of the hometown weekly. It said:

FORTUNE INVESTIGATIONS
12 Main Street, East Plainfield. 732-555-6061
Competent—Caring—Discreet

Maybe it was a long shot, but it was a step in the right direction. Ed Fortune had always been all about advertising. She didn't expect miracles, but at least it might make her phone ring a bit more.

"Dad would like to see this," she murmured, running her finger over the newsprint.

As she went to grab a pair of scissors to cut the ad out, someone knocked on the door. When she went to open it, she was surprised to see a solid, compact man with a goatee, and a bit of a red, shiny forehead. It was Zachary Hardy.

"Oh, hello," she said, astonished. "What are you doing here?"

He laughed. "I've been living in the states for the past decade," he said with a smile. "My home base is Philadelphia."

She blinked. "But I thought you and your father—"

"My father runs the business overseas. I've only been over there to help him out, when necessary," he explained, looking past her. "Might I come in?"

"Sure. Of course," she said, remembering her dinner, which was still in the carton near the couch. "I was just eating. Did you want some—"

"No, actually. I just stopped by to see how you were doing."

"Good."

"That was some case. And the way you solved it? I don't think I've ever had so much excitement in my life. It was pretty impressive."

"Ah. Thanks." She blushed.

"And your head is better?"

"Fine, fine," she said, looking around, wishing she could think of something interesting to say. "And how are you?"

"Just great. I also wanted to . . . well . . . ask if you'd ever want to, I don't know, accompany me to dinner sometime?"

"Oh, uh . . ." Again, she was speechless. Was this a romantic overture? Her mind had been so wrapped up in the case, she hadn't thought about him in that way at all. "I . . ."

He held up a hand. "Don't worry." He reached into the pocket of his blazer and pulled out a business card. "If you ever want to meet up, give me a call."

She stared at the business card, then nodded. "I can do that."

He continued to smile at her for almost a beat too long, and then suddenly jumped to action. "Well, I won't disturb you any longer. Take care, Daisy."

She walked him to the door, waved, and closed it, then leaned against it and sighed. *Could you possibly be any more awkward, Daisy?*

As she was rolling her eyes at herself, they landed on a photograph on the mantle of her fireplace. She walked slowly over to it, taking in the individual people in it. Her father, her mother, who'd died when she was a child, and Charlie, her older brother.

Hard to believe he'd been gone almost twenty years.

In the world of the rich and famous, a world where it was so important to keep secrets and stay discreet, he had fallen between the cracks. Ed Fortune had gone crazy trying to find out what had happened to him, but he simply hadn't had the resources. He'd run into stone walls, everywhere he went.

Maybe, if she went to the Caribbean, she'd have a chance to tear some of those walls down.

NOW AVAILABLE!

CLAIM YOU
(A Daisy Fortune Mystery—Book 2)

Brilliant private investigator Daisy Fortune is known for cracking cases in the opaque world of the uber-wealthy, but when a new case lands—a wealthy tycoon found dead on his private jet in Monaco—even Daisy is stumped. Yet as she unearths his darkest secrets and meets all the hangers-on in his life, even Daisy cannot anticipate what she will discover.

"A masterpiece of thriller and mystery."
—Books and Movie Reviews, Roberto Mattos (re Once Gone)

CLAIM YOU is Book #2 in a long-anticipated new series by #1 bestseller and USA Today bestselling author Blake Pierce, whose bestseller Once Gone (a free download) has received over 7,000 five star ratings and reviews.

Daisy Fortune never wanted to be a private investigator, but when her father had a stroke, she felt obliged to carry on the family business. Her P.I. business is on the brink of bankruptcy when an uber-wealthy client offers an extraordinary fee to clear her name. To do so, Daisy will have to immerse herself in the world of the mega-rich—a world Daisy knows nothing of.

Red flags abound as Daisy finds herself pulled deeper into the web of lies and dark secrets of the world's wealthiest.

Secrets they will do anything to protect.

Daisy, though, is brilliant and tenacious, and as she steps into the role, she begins to realize she has her father's gift. Unearthing the truth becomes a passion for her and she learns she will stop at nothing to do it—even if it means risking her own life.

A page-turning private investigator thriller, the DAISY FORTUNE series is a riveting mystery, featuring a brilliant detective and packed with non-stop action, suspense, twists and turns, revelations, and driven by a breakneck pace that will keep you flipping pages late into the night. Fans of Michael Connelly, Harlan Coben and L.T. Ryan are sure to fall in love.

Future books in the series are also now available.

"An edge of your seat thriller in a new series that keeps you turning pages! ...So many twists, turns and red herrings… I can't wait to see what happens next."
—Reader review (Her Last Wish)

"A strong, complex story about two FBI agents trying to stop a serial killer. If you want an author to capture your attention and have you guessing, yet trying to put the pieces together, Pierce is your author!"
—Reader review (Her Last Wish)

"A typical Blake Pierce twisting, turning, roller coaster ride suspense thriller. Will have you turning the pages to the last sentence of the last chapter!!!"
—Reader review (City of Prey)

"Right from the start we have an unusual protagonist that I haven't seen done in this genre before. The action is nonstop… A very atmospheric novel that will keep you turning pages well into the wee hours."
—Reader review (City of Prey)

"Everything that I look for in a book… a great plot, interesting characters, and grabs your interest right away. The book moves along at a breakneck pace and stays that way until the end. Now on go I to book two!"
—Reader review (Girl, Alone)

"Exciting, heart pounding, edge of your seat book… a must read for mystery and suspense readers!"
—Reader review (Girl, Alone)

Blake Pierce

Blake Pierce is the USA Today bestselling author of the RILEY PAGE mystery series, which includes seventeen books. Blake Pierce is also the author of the MACKENZIE WHITE mystery series, comprising fourteen books; of the AVERY BLACK mystery series, comprising six books; of the KERI LOCKE mystery series, comprising five books; of the MAKING OF RILEY PAIGE mystery series, comprising six books; of the KATE WISE mystery series, comprising seven books; of the CHLOE FINE psychological suspense mystery, comprising six books; of the JESSIE HUNT psychological suspense thriller series, comprising twenty six books; of the AU PAIR psychological suspense thriller series, comprising three books; of the ZOE PRIME mystery series, comprising six books; of the ADELE SHARP mystery series, comprising sixteen books, of the EUROPEAN VOYAGE cozy mystery series, comprising six books; of the LAURA FROST FBI suspense thriller, comprising eleven books; of the ELLA DARK FBI suspense thriller, comprising fourteen books (and counting); of the A YEAR IN EUROPE cozy mystery series, comprising nine books, of the AVA GOLD mystery series, comprising six books; of the RACHEL GIFT mystery series, comprising ten books (and counting); of the VALERIE LAW mystery series, comprising nine books (and counting); of the PAIGE KING mystery series, comprising eight books (and counting); of the MAY MOORE mystery series, comprising eleven books (and counting); the CORA SHIELDS mystery series, comprising five books (and counting); of the NICKY LYONS mystery series, comprising seven books (and counting), of the CAMI LARK mystery series, comprising five books (and counting), of the AMBER YOUNG mystery series, comprising five books (and counting), of the DAISY FORTUNE mystery series, comprising five books (and counting), and of the new FIONA RED mystery series, comprising five books (and counting).

An avid reader and lifelong fan of the mystery and thriller genres, Blake loves to hear from you, so please feel free to visit www.blakepierceauthor.com to learn more and stay in touch.

BOOKS BY BLAKE PIERCE

FIONA RED MYSTERY SERIES

LET HER GO (Book #1)
LET HER BE (Book #2)
LET HER HOPE (Book #3)
LET HER WISH (Book #4)
LET HER LIVE (Book #5)

DAISY FORTUNE MYSTERY SERIES

NEED YOU (Book #1)
CLAIM YOU (Book #2)
CRAVE YOU (Book #3)
CHOOSE YOU (Book #4)
CHASE YOU (Book #5)

AMBER YOUNG MYSTERY SERIES

ABSENT PITY (Book #1)
ABSENT REMORSE (Book #2)
ABSENT FEELING (Book #3)
ABSENT MERCY (Book #4)
ABSENT REASON (Book #5)

CAMI LARK MYSTERY SERIES

JUST ME (Book #1)
JUST OUTSIDE (Book #2)
JUST RIGHT (Book #3)
JUST FORGET (Book #4)
JUST ONCE (Book #5)

NICKY LYONS MYSTERY SERIES

ALL MINE (Book #1)
ALL HIS (Book #2)
ALL HE SEES (Book #3)
ALL ALONE (Book #4)
ALL FOR ONE (Book #5)

ALL HE TAKES (Book #6)
ALL FOR ME (Book #7)

CORA SHIELDS MYSTERY SERIES
UNDONE (Book #1)
UNWANTED (Book #2)
UNHINGED (Book #3)
UNSAID (Book #4)
UNGLUED (Book #5)

MAY MOORE SUSPENSE THRILLER
NEVER RUN (Book #1)
NEVER TELL (Book #2)
NEVER LIVE (Book #3)
NEVER HIDE (Book #4)
NEVER FORGIVE (Book #5)
NEVER AGAIN (Book #6)
NEVER LOOK BACK (Book #7)
NEVER FORGET (Book #8)
NEVER LET GO (Book #9)
NEVER PRETEND (Book #10)
NEVER HESITATE (Book #11)

PAIGE KING MYSTERY SERIES
THE GIRL HE PINED (Book #1)
THE GIRL HE CHOSE (Book #2)
THE GIRL HE TOOK (Book #3)
THE GIRL HE WISHED (Book #4)
THE GIRL HE CROWNED (Book #5)
THE GIRL HE WATCHED (Book #6)
THE GIRL HE WANTED (Book #7)
THE GIRL HE CLAIMED (Book #8)

VALERIE LAW MYSTERY SERIES
NO MERCY (Book #1)
NO PITY (Book #2)
NO FEAR (Book #3)
NO SLEEP (Book #4)
NO QUARTER (Book #5)

NO CHANCE (Book #6)
NO REFUGE (Book #7)
NO GRACE (Book #8)
NO ESCAPE (Book #9)

RACHEL GIFT MYSTERY SERIES
HER LAST WISH (Book #1)
HER LAST CHANCE (Book #2)
HER LAST HOPE (Book #3)
HER LAST FEAR (Book #4)
HER LAST CHOICE (Book #5)
HER LAST BREATH (Book #6)
HER LAST MISTAKE (Book #7)
HER LAST DESIRE (Book #8)
HER LAST REGRET (Book #9)
HER LAST HOUR (Book #10)

AVA GOLD MYSTERY SERIES
CITY OF PREY (Book #1)
CITY OF FEAR (Book #2)
CITY OF BONES (Book #3)
CITY OF GHOSTS (Book #4)
CITY OF DEATH (Book #5)
CITY OF VICE (Book #6)

A YEAR IN EUROPE
A MURDER IN PARIS (Book #1)
DEATH IN FLORENCE (Book #2)
VENGEANCE IN VIENNA (Book #3)
A FATALITY IN SPAIN (Book #4)

ELLA DARK FBI SUSPENSE THRILLER
GIRL, ALONE (Book #1)
GIRL, TAKEN (Book #2)
GIRL, HUNTED (Book #3)
GIRL, SILENCED (Book #4)
GIRL, VANISHED (Book 5)
GIRL ERASED (Book #6)
GIRL, FORSAKEN (Book #7)

GIRL, TRAPPED (Book #8)
GIRL, EXPENDABLE (Book #9)
GIRL, ESCAPED (Book #10)
GIRL, HIS (Book #11)
GIRL, LURED (Book #12)
GIRL, MISSING (Book #13)
GIRL, UNKNOWN (Book #14)

LAURA FROST FBI SUSPENSE THRILLER
ALREADY GONE (Book #1)
ALREADY SEEN (Book #2)
ALREADY TRAPPED (Book #3)
ALREADY MISSING (Book #4)
ALREADY DEAD (Book #5)
ALREADY TAKEN (Book #6)
ALREADY CHOSEN (Book #7)
ALREADY LOST (Book #8)
ALREADY HIS (Book #9)
ALREADY LURED (Book #10)
ALREADY COLD (Book #11)

EUROPEAN VOYAGE COZY MYSTERY SERIES
MURDER (AND BAKLAVA) (Book #1)
DEATH (AND APPLE STRUDEL) (Book #2)
CRIME (AND LAGER) (Book #3)
MISFORTUNE (AND GOUDA) (Book #4)
CALAMITY (AND A DANISH) (Book #5)
MAYHEM (AND HERRING) (Book #6)

ADELE SHARP MYSTERY SERIES
LEFT TO DIE (Book #1)
LEFT TO RUN (Book #2)
LEFT TO HIDE (Book #3)
LEFT TO KILL (Book #4)
LEFT TO MURDER (Book #5)
LEFT TO ENVY (Book #6)
LEFT TO LAPSE (Book #7)
LEFT TO VANISH (Book #8)
LEFT TO HUNT (Book #9)

LEFT TO FEAR (Book #10)
LEFT TO PREY (Book #11)
LEFT TO LURE (Book #12)
LEFT TO CRAVE (Book #13)
LEFT TO LOATHE (Book #14)
LEFT TO HARM (Book #15)
LEFT TO RUIN (Book #16)

THE AU PAIR SERIES
ALMOST GONE (Book#1)
ALMOST LOST (Book #2)
ALMOST DEAD (Book #3)

ZOE PRIME MYSTERY SERIES
FACE OF DEATH (Book#1)
FACE OF MURDER (Book #2)
FACE OF FEAR (Book #3)
FACE OF MADNESS (Book #4)
FACE OF FURY (Book #5)
FACE OF DARKNESS (Book #6)

A JESSIE HUNT PSYCHOLOGICAL SUSPENSE SERIES
THE PERFECT WIFE (Book #1)
THE PERFECT BLOCK (Book #2)
THE PERFECT HOUSE (Book #3)
THE PERFECT SMILE (Book #4)
THE PERFECT LIE (Book #5)
THE PERFECT LOOK (Book #6)
THE PERFECT AFFAIR (Book #7)
THE PERFECT ALIBI (Book #8)
THE PERFECT NEIGHBOR (Book #9)
THE PERFECT DISGUISE (Book #10)
THE PERFECT SECRET (Book #11)
THE PERFECT FAÇADE (Book #12)
THE PERFECT IMPRESSION (Book #13)
THE PERFECT DECEIT (Book #14)
THE PERFECT MISTRESS (Book #15)
THE PERFECT IMAGE (Book #16)
THE PERFECT VEIL (Book #17)

THE PERFECT INDISCRETION (Book #18)
THE PERFECT RUMOR (Book #19)
THE PERFECT COUPLE (Book #20)
THE PERFECT MURDER (Book #21)
THE PERFECT HUSBAND (Book #22)
THE PERFECT SCANDAL (Book #23)
THE PERFECT MASK (Book #24)
THE PERFECT RUSE (Book #25)
THE PERFECT VENEER (Book #26)

CHLOE FINE PSYCHOLOGICAL SUSPENSE SERIES
NEXT DOOR (Book #1)
A NEIGHBOR'S LIE (Book #2)
CUL DE SAC (Book #3)
SILENT NEIGHBOR (Book #4)
HOMECOMING (Book #5)
TINTED WINDOWS (Book #6)

KATE WISE MYSTERY SERIES
IF SHE KNEW (Book #1)
IF SHE SAW (Book #2)
IF SHE RAN (Book #3)
IF SHE HID (Book #4)
IF SHE FLED (Book #5)
IF SHE FEARED (Book #6)
IF SHE HEARD (Book #7)

THE MAKING OF RILEY PAIGE SERIES
WATCHING (Book #1)
WAITING (Book #2)
LURING (Book #3)
TAKING (Book #4)
STALKING (Book #5)
KILLING (Book #6)

RILEY PAIGE MYSTERY SERIES
ONCE GONE (Book #1)
ONCE TAKEN (Book #2)
ONCE CRAVED (Book #3)

ONCE LURED (Book #4)
ONCE HUNTED (Book #5)
ONCE PINED (Book #6)
ONCE FORSAKEN (Book #7)
ONCE COLD (Book #8)
ONCE STALKED (Book #9)
ONCE LOST (Book #10)
ONCE BURIED (Book #11)
ONCE BOUND (Book #12)
ONCE TRAPPED (Book #13)
ONCE DORMANT (Book #14)
ONCE SHUNNED (Book #15)
ONCE MISSED (Book #16)
ONCE CHOSEN (Book #17)

MACKENZIE WHITE MYSTERY SERIES
BEFORE HE KILLS (Book #1)
BEFORE HE SEES (Book #2)
BEFORE HE COVETS (Book #3)
BEFORE HE TAKES (Book #4)
BEFORE HE NEEDS (Book #5)
BEFORE HE FEELS (Book #6)
BEFORE HE SINS (Book #7)
BEFORE HE HUNTS (Book #8)
BEFORE HE PREYS (Book #9)
BEFORE HE LONGS (Book #10)
BEFORE HE LAPSES (Book #11)
BEFORE HE ENVIES (Book #12)
BEFORE HE STALKS (Book #13)
BEFORE HE HARMS (Book #14)

AVERY BLACK MYSTERY SERIES
CAUSE TO KILL (Book #1)
CAUSE TO RUN (Book #2)
CAUSE TO HIDE (Book #3)
CAUSE TO FEAR (Book #4)
CAUSE TO SAVE (Book #5)
CAUSE TO DREAD (Book #6)

KERI LOCKE MYSTERY SERIES

A TRACE OF DEATH (Book #1)
A TRACE OF MURDER (Book #2)
A TRACE OF VICE (Book #3)
A TRACE OF CRIME (Book #4)
A TRACE OF HOPE (Book #5)

Made in the USA
Coppell, TX
09 February 2023

12549177R00099